COBBLE BAY

BY: Sandra Capwell

PROLOGUE:

Abby Sampson had endured many years of an unhappy marriage. Her husband had become withdrawn from his family. His only interest was his position at the bank. Abby managed to raise her children without the presence of their father for all notable events in their young lives.

When Joseph dies suddenly, she must find a new life for herself. Her children are grown with their own families. They remain a large part of Abby's life but eventually she finds she has passions that are pulling her in a different direction.

When she decides to finally have a career, she is excited. However, she did not expect the career to include a new love interest. She finds herself attracted to Jefferson Matthews and is shocked when she realizes the feelings are mutual.

Their life together begins with a mystery. It draws them closer while they try to find a solution to this unexpected event.

While Abby tries to open her heart to Jefferson, she must try to persuade her children that he is the right choice for her. Her daughter stands behind her mother's choices but winning her son over to the prospect of having a stepfather is not an easy task.

The village of Cobble Bay and its citizens play a large part in the development of this new romance.

CHAPTER ONE:

Abigail Sampson sat on the porch looking out over the bay below. She loved this time of year. The leaves were turning, and the air was cool coming in off the water. The autumn in New England was always a glorious burst of colors. Orange and red dotted the trees on the front lawn. She wondered if the children would be late driving in from Bar Harbor. The weekend traffic was always heavy this time of the year. The tourists would flock north to witness the leaves changing. They would stop in Freeport to shop at the outlets and then venture further to Bar Harbor or one of the other coastal towns.

She was glad she had kept the house after Joseph died. Her children thought she might sell and find something smaller. She however was looking ahead for the time when they would all visit with their own families. That time had come as they had both married and had started to give her grandchildren. She enjoyed being a young grandmother. She loved the noise and chaos the youngsters would bring to the old house. It reminded her of when her children were growing up. There would always be a houseful of other children every day after school and on weekends. They all seemed to gather at her home. It was the fact that she was home waiting for the school bus to arrive. Maybe it was just the freshly baked cookies and glasses of milk they always found ready for them.

Whatever the reason, she was always pleased to see a few extra kids step down off the bus with her children. She would give them snacks in the large kitchen and then watch as they all sat around the table doing their homework. Their parents were always calling and apologizing to her about the extra children. She always told them it was no bother. In fact, she enjoyed their company as much as her children did.

Her days were quiet otherwise. Once the children had left for school and her husband Joseph had left for the office, the big house seemed quite lonely at times. She would always keep busy cleaning and doing the laundry. Joseph enjoyed a huge meal every evening so she would plan her menu daily. If she needed any extra ingredients, she would take a short drive to the local market. Joseph kept her on a tight budget, and she had to account for the money she spent every week.

He took care of paying the bills and always managed their bank accounts. She never actually saw his paycheck and had no idea how much money he made at his job. It was not until his death that she saw the finances. She was shocked to find out how much he had put away in a savings account. The account was just in his name of course, but since everything was left to her in the will, she had no trouble accessing the money he had saved.

He had purchased a sizeable insurance policy after her pleading. Along with his pension money she was able to keep the house and provide for her children. He had specified an amount to be put into accounts for both the children for college funds. Her son had taken advantage of that when he finished high school. He had plans to become an engineer and attended Boston University for four years.

Her daughter preferred to attend the local culinary school. After graduating she was hired by a local restaurant. After a year she moved away to Bar Harbor and was head chef at one of their more prestigious restaurants.

Both of her children had dated during college and married shortly after they graduated.

Her son, Henry, now had a son who was three years old and a daughter who was almost two months old. Her daughter, Cassie had married a boy she had known her entire life. They wanted to start a family, but their life was so demanding with their jobs that it had not happened yet.

Abby's life with Joseph had not been a particularly happy one. He was not the type of man who showed his feelings in public to her or their children. When they were alone, he acted the same way most of the time except when his sexual urges kicked in. Then it was all about his needs and he never bothered to worry about hers.

Abby had grown up with two loving parents who were always hugging and kissing each other. They had no trouble showing her the same affection. When she met Joseph, he acted quite different towards her. He was loving and made a big production of pleasing her. Once they were married, he changed into a different man.

He was always very demanding of Abby. He had told her he did not want her to have a career. He wanted her to remain home and care for his needs. He was attending medical school when they met. He worked at the local hospital for some time and then was made director. The job took all his time. He expected the house to be spotless and dinner to be on the table when he arrived home in the evening. He was not pleased with Abby when she told him she was pregnant with their son. He had not wanted children.

She was pleased that he had provided financial security for her and the children. They had not received much attention or affection from Joseph. They knew better than to disturb their father. They had Abby and that was all they needed.

CHAPTER TWO:

Abby thought about her recent purchase. She wondered what the children would have to say about the antique shop she decided to buy. They had always known her as a mother who did not work.

 After Joseph died and Abby was made aware of their financial situation, she began to think of a life change. She had followed Joseph's wishes during their marriage and stayed at home. She had dreams of having her own career, but never mentioned them to Joseph. She knew what his response would be and decided it was not worth upsetting him.

She was content raising the children, however when they began school the house started to close in on her at times. She tried to approach the subject of getting a job with Joseph, but he just told her she was not qualified for anything so why bother. He told her that his position at the hospital afforded them enough income that she did not need to find employment.

Abby tried to make him understand that it was not for the money, but to give her some purpose in her life. Joseph would just laugh and tell her that was a ridiculous notion. "You have me to take care of and our children. Why would you want to upset our household by getting a job?" She would take his statements as probably true. She had married young and did not have the education he possessed. She pushed the idea out of her head and spent her days as usual, cleaning and cooking for Joseph. Being at home when her children returned from school did give her immense pleasure, but she still longed for more.

The day she had noticed the sign in the window of the antique shop, she had been curious. She had looked through the store a few times and loved browsing through all the older items. She went inside and the clerk approached her. "Can I help you find anything in particular?" he asked. Abby shook her head no. "I wanted to inquire about your sign. Your shop is for sale?"

The clerk smiled at her and said he would get the owner. As she waited, she looked around at some of the furniture. She noticed quite a few beautiful pieces that she thought would look lovely in her home.

When the owner walked up to her, she was surprised to see someone so young. She assumed the owner would be elderly. "Hello. I understand you are interested in our for-sale sign," he said as he smiled at Abby. "Yes. I have browsed in your shop a few times and was surprised to see you were selling." He asked her to follow him to his office and she saw the clerk watching as they walked to the back of the store.

"Please, have a seat Mrs.?" Abby looked at him as she settled into the chair in front of his desk. "Oh, I am sorry. My name is Abigail Sampson." He listened as she spoke and did not answer right away. "Very nice to make your acquaintance," he finally said. "My name is Jefferson Matthews."

He proceeded to tell her about the shop. She listened to his slightly British accent and learned the shop had been in his family for quite some time. He had stepped in to run the shop recently after his father had passed away suddenly.

"Oh, I am sorry for your loss," she replied. He smiled and nodded. "Thank you. Now what makes you think you would enjoy owning an antique shop? Have you worked in one before?" Abby told him she had not held a job since she was a teenager. She told him her husband had passed away and her children were grown with their own families.

"I have been wanting to find something to fill my days. I have always loved the items you have in your shop. In fact, I saw a few today that would be lovely additions to my home. My husband owned quite a few antique pieces of furniture that had belonged to his parents. He taught me how to care for them and gave me some lessons in the history of antique items. I think he would have liked to know the money he left me would be invested in something he was passionate about."

Jefferson was very attentive to her explanation. He took a few moments before he made any comments. When he did, Abby was amazed at his response. "My father left me the shop in his will. However, there was a stipulation to his bequeath. If I did not want to continue running the shop, I could sell it on one condition. I had to find someone who had the same passion as he did for beautiful antique items and furniture. Mrs. Sampson, I am beginning to believe you just might be that person."

Abby smiled and told him she would treat the shop as his father would have. She would take care of the items inside as if they were her own. "I tell you what I will do. How does this sound to you?" He proceeded to tell Abby that if she would agree to work in the shop for a month, he could better access her ability and interest to purchase the property and its contents.

Abby thought about his offer for a brief time. "Mr. Matthews. You have yourself a deal. This way it will give us both time to decide if this venture is the best for both of us."

He stood and reached his hand out to her. When Abby took his hand and they shook, she could not help but notice how smooth his skin was. She assumed he was someone who had not done hard labor in his life. At least not recently.

When she walked out of the shop, she felt excited about her new endeavor. By the time, she got to her car, she realized they had not spoken about the price he was asking for the shop. She assumed they would discuss that when she returned to start working the following week.

She drove home smiling and humming to herself. She was finally doing something for herself. Something for her future. She did not have the slightest doubt in her mind about her decision. The moment she had stepped inside the shop, she had felt like she belonged there.

CHAPTER THREE:

The next few days seemed to take forever. Abby was so excited about getting to the shop. She looked through her wardrobe and decided on a dark green suit and white blouse. She remembered how handsomely dressed Mr. Matthews had been. The clerk followed the same dress code. She did not want to appear too casual with her attire.

She decided to go to her hairdresser and get a new hairdo. Something that looked more businesslike. She had always worn her hair long since that is what Joseph preferred. Even though he never commented about her looks.

The day finally arrived, and Abby was up before the sunrise. She had found it hard to sleep with thinking about the approaching day. She dressed carefully and approved of her reflection in the hall mirror as she came down the stairs.

"I may not fit Mr. Matthews image of a shop owner for my ability. At least I can look the part. Then I can persuade him of the other requirements to purchase his shop."

The drive to town only took Abby a few moments. Cobble Bay did not have a lot of traffic. Most of the people worked on the docks and they all started their days much earlier. She saw most of the boats had left the harbor as she drove past the marina.

She pulled into a parking space in front of the shop. The lights were already on inside. She worried that she was late but found the door to be locked when she turned the knob.

Abby knocked on the door and waited for only a few minutes before she saw Mr. Matthews walking toward her. "Well, good morning Mrs. Sampson. Bright and early, I see." She smiled as she followed him inside. "Please Mr. Matthews, call me Abby." He nodded at her. "Well, then my name is Jefferson." He waited for her as he walked to the rear of the shop.

He told her the clerk usually arrived at nine. "I try to get in early to do whatever paperwork I did not finish the day before. The bank deposit is made every day first thing. My clerk walks it over to the bank across the street after he arrives. That will be one of the tasks I give to you after a few days. This way the clerk can concentrate on any early customers we might have. The business is not too busy this time of the week. Most of the tourists are in town on the weekends. There are some locals that frequent the shop. You will get to know them as the time passes. I have a feeling the word will get out about a possible new owner. They will all want to see what you look like. Small town. I am sure you are used to people being inquisitive about any changes in town."

Abby told him she had been a homemaker and mother for many years. She did not know too many residents of the town. Those that had small children who grew up with hers was the main part of the town residents that she knew.

The day proceeded as Abby expected. The clerk came into the shop right at nine. Jefferson gave him the bank bag and they watched as he crossed the street. It was only a few minutes before he returned to the shop. He gave the bag and receipts to Jefferson and went to the front of the shop. There were no customers, so he started to clean and arrange the furniture and items that were for sale.

The morning went by faster than Abby thought it would. The few customers that came in were taken care of professionally by George, the clerk. Jefferson told her George had worked in the store when his father was alive. Abby thought that was the case because of George's obvious advanced years.

She observed when he would greet a customer. He was very businesslike but friendly to everyone. Most of the customers were just browsing and he would watch from a distance as they walked among the many pieces of furniture. He would make himself available if they had any questions but did not hover over them. Abby knew how that made them feel more comfortable and made the possibility of a sale much better. She knew from her own experience. Make your presence known to the customer but do not follow them around. They would let you know if they found something interesting to them. Be close, but not too close was a particularly good tactic on George's part, she thought.

Jefferson came over to her while she was helping George tidy a nearby display. "It is lunchtime Abigail. We close the shop from noon til one thirty. I usually walk to the cafe down the street if you would like to join me." She thanked him for the invitation and got her purse from behind the counter.

She saw George walk into the back room with his lunch bag. "He has always brought his brown bag lunch for as long as I can remember," Jefferson said. Abby walked down the street with Jefferson. She noticed a few of the other shop owners looking out their windows and watching. She looked at Jefferson and he smiled down at her. "I told you. Small town." She nodded and they proceeded to the café.

Abby followed Jefferson to an empty booth and sat down across from him. The waitress came over and greeted him by name. She looked over at Abby but made no comment about who she was. Abby chose the soup of the day and Jefferson asked for the same. When the waitress had delivered their drinks, Jefferson looked around the room.

"Not too busy today. I am sure that Sally has already alerted everyone to the fact I have company today." It seemed no sooner than he had made his observation that people started to enter the café. They all looked over and said hello to Jefferson.

He did not say anything to her, but just smiled and nodded to the newcomers. Abby wondered who the others thought she was. Possibly a personal acquaintance of Jefferson. For a fleeting moment, she thought that would be something she found pleasing. Jefferson was tall and quite good looking. He carried himself like someone who had a lot of confidence. The difference between him and her late husband was his attitude. Abby sensed there was a quiet, but pleasant man behind that smile. He had confidence but not arrogance. When he spoke to the waitress he did not appear to look down on her for her menial job. Abby did not remember his father but felt like he had learned how to act at an early age.

Their soup arrived and they ate without conversation. She looked around the room occasionally and saw the customers only glanced towards them a few times. Finally, Jefferson looked up from his lunch, "I am sorry. I did not take time for breakfast today and I was quite hungry. I am usually a better luncheon companion."

"Oh, that is fine. I am enjoying my soup. That is one thing I have always loved about living here. The local cuisine is always delicious." Jefferson agreed with her and asked if she had eaten out a lot when her husband was alive. "No, not really. Joseph always preferred dinner at home after work. He would attend some dinners at the local restaurants for his position at the hospital. I would always stay home with the children. He did not approve of babysitters."

Jefferson did not comment but had a look on his face that said a lot. As he listened to Abigail, he wondered what kind of man she had married. It sounded like he had been very controlling. She was such an attractive woman. Why wouldn't he want to show her off to his colleagues.

They finished their lunch and after Jefferson paid the check, he held the door for Abby. The walk back to the shop was quiet again. She did not see any of the shop keepers watching this time. Perhaps Sally had filled them in on any conversation she had overheard.

CHAPTER FOUR:

The remainder of the afternoon was spent observing George with the customers. Jefferson told her to help if she was needed. He wanted to get a sense of how she would be in the shop. He already thought she was the person he was looking for, but he did not want to be too quick with his decision. She would have appealed to his father, he was certain.

John Matthews had always been particularly good at sizing up people. Jefferson remembered when he was a young boy and spent time in the shop with his father. He had been impressed his father could tell if the customer would buy something or not.

His father had been well-liked and respected in Cobble Bay. John had always wanted his son to continue running the family business. He was sad to learn when Jefferson got older and graduated from college that he wanted to see the world. He never held his son back from traveling but was always glad when he returned home.

When John had gotten ill in his older years, Jefferson would spend longer periods in Cobble Bay. He did love the town and he loved his father even more. He had lost his mother when he was in his teens and his father stepped in to fill both parents' positions.

He had been a loving father to Jefferson. The cancer worked too fast on John, and he was gone before Jefferson was ready to say goodbye. The shop had been in the family so long that Jefferson felt obligated to continue running the business. He knew how much his father loved the shop and when he read the will John had left, he understood his father's wishes completely.

Abby found herself enjoying the shop even more than she had expected. When closing time arrived, she almost hated to leave. Jefferson and George closed the shop and they told her they would see her the next day.

She watched as they walked to their cars that were parked nearby. As she drove through the streets towards home, she felt incredibly pleased with herself. She knew her decision had been the right one. She only hoped Jefferson felt the same way.

Pulling in her drive she noticed a package on the front porch. Coming up the steps she saw the return address. It was from her daughter Cassie.

Abby carried the box inside and before she had a chance to open it the phone began to ring. Cassie's name came up on the caller ID. "Hi sweetheart. How are you?" Her daughter's voice sounded strange, but happy. "Hi Mom. I am fine thanks. You?" Abby told her she was good and asked about the package she was still holding.

"Why don't you just open it, Mom." said Cassie. Abby put her phone on speaker and tore open the wrapping. Inside the box was a lot of tissue. When she pulled it all away, she found a small onesie inscribed with the word "Grandma's little love."

Abby gasped and yelled to her daughter on the phone. "Cassie. Does this mean what I think?" She could hear her daughter's voice and knew her daughter was crying just as she was. "Yes Mom. We are pregnant at last."

The conversation continued with all the details. Cassie and her husband Jake had only found out a few days before. She had bought the gift for her mother even before her doctor appointment to verify the pregnancy. Both women laughed and cried together for quite some time.

Abby could hear her son-in-law's voice in the background. "What do you think Grandma? Ready for more additions to the family?" he asked. Abby told them both how happy she was for them. She knew how much they had wanted a baby and she thought the news was the most wonderful thing that had happened all day.

Of course, she knew her news was wonderful too, but this was her daughter's moment. She talked for a brief time and then Cassie had to go because the restaurant was getting busy.

Abby made sure the plans were still in place for a big family dinner. Cassie told her mother they had the manager covering the restaurant for the weekend and she was looking forward to seeing her mother and brother.

After she hung up the call, she sat at the kitchen table and looked at the tiny onesie in her hands. A new baby. She loved the idea. She knew her daughter was going to make a wonderful mother. She looked around the kitchen and thought to herself what an amazing day it had been. She could not wait until she saw her children to tell them about the antique shop. Of course, she hoped the shop would be hers by that time, but if not, she could at least convince Jefferson to let her work there whenever he was not in town.

CHAPTER FIVE:

Abby was up early again the next day. After breakfast, she was anxious to get to the shop. She stopped at the local bakery and purchased a dozen freshly baked cookies for the store.

She arrived at the shop as Jefferson was unlocking the front door. He saw her pull into the parking lot next to the shop and waited for her. "Good morning, Abby. It looks like another beautiful fall day," Jefferson said as he held the door for her. "What do you have in the box?" She smiled and told him she had stopped at the bakery. "Oh, did a little bird tell you I skipped breakfast again?" He laughed and took the box that she handed to him.

"Oh, I love that bakery. Their pastries are delicious. My father would stop on the way home from the shop when I was a child. He would always bring me home my favorites, chocolate chip cookies." Abby smiled with his comment and watched as he opened the box. "Well, it looks like that little bird really hit the nail on the head," he remarked as he laughed and took a cookie.

"It looks like our minds are on the same wavelength today," Abby said. He nodded with his mouth full of the warm cookie. She followed him into the office and watched as he took the bank bag out of the safe behind his desk. "How about you walk along with George this morning to the bank. That way you will see what he does, and you can take over the duties tomorrow." Abby agreed.

Jefferson was quiet for a few minutes. "I did not think about mentioning it yesterday, but I like your new hairdo. It is very becoming. You have a small face, and the shorter style really complements you.

Abby thanked him for the compliment and tried not to blush. She was so used to Joseph not noticing her hair or clothes. It seemed strange to receive a compliment, but very pleasant indeed.

George came in the door before she had time to say anything else to Jefferson. He instructed George that Abby would accompany him to the bank. George said nothing, but just nodded and took the bank bag from Jefferson. He held the door for Abby as they walked out of the shop.

Abby hoped that George did not think she was overstepping his duties with the shop. "I love this fall weather." she remarked. George did not answer, but just shook his head in agreement.

When they walked up to the teller at the bank, Abby stood aside and watched as George handed her the bag. She was surprised when he spoke to the teller, "This is Mrs. Sampson. She will be bringing the bank bag over in the morning starting tomorrow." The teller smiled at Abby and nodded.

The transaction only took a few minutes to complete. Abby followed George outside and across to the shop. When they were inside, George handed her the empty bag, and he went over to the front counter to begin his daily cleaning.

Abby walked back to the office and gave the bag to Jefferson. "I hope George is not bothered by me taking over his bank duties," she said to Jefferson. He smiled at her. "I am certain he is not. He would much rather come in and begin cleaning and straightening our merchandise.

After my father got too ill and I started filling in, I would take the bank deposits to the bank. I decided to give the task to George, and he never really appreciated the added responsibility. He does not speak much, but last night when we were walking to our cars, he did mention he thought you were a nice addition to our shop.

Abby was surprised at Jefferson's remark. She had thought George was feeling just the opposite. She smiled and walked out to the front of the shop to assist George with some customers.

Jefferson sat at his desk watching her. "Yes, father. Abby is going to be exactly the person you were hoping for. I cannot wait to see her face though when we discuss the financial terms of the sale." He continued to smile and took another cookie from the box before starting his paperwork.

CHAPTER SIX:

The customers were much more plentiful as the morning went on. Abby was able to take care of a couple that were looking at a particularly large buffet table. She listened as they explained their dining room and exactly how well the table would look with their other furniture.

She asked George for some assistance with their questions about delivery. After answering their questions, George told Abby she could complete the sale and walked over to some others who had entered the shop.

Jefferson seemed pleased with the sale when she handed him the customer's check. "That is one piece we have had in the store for quite some time. I knew there was someone who would find it exactly right for their home. I am pleased you were able to convince them."

Abby completed the sale and walked the customers to the door. They thanked her for her help and said they could not wait until the piece was delivered to their house. Abby felt immensely proud of herself and spent the remainder of the morning helping George rearrange some other items to fill in the empty spot where the buffet had stood. Jefferson announced he was leaving for lunch shortly after noon. He asked Abby if she would like to join him. She thanked him for the invitation but said she had brought her lunch. She wanted to spend some time alone with George. After Jefferson left and George locked the front door, she followed him to the back room. There was a small refrigerator and microwave. The table was small, but beautiful. Abby sat after getting her lunch out of the fridge. George remained quiet for a time. She watched as he pulled a napkin from his bag and placed it on the table. Then he took a sandwich out and placed it on the napkin.

They sat quietly eating for a few minutes. "I hope you do not mind my company today, George. I had leftovers from my dinner and decided they would be good for lunch." He looked at her and smiled. "Mrs. Sampson, I do not mind at all. It is nice to have someone to chat with during lunch. Mr. Jefferson likes to get out of the shop each day, but I love my time here."

Abby nodded, "Yes, I agree with you. This shop is special. I really enjoyed my day yesterday. And my name is Abby." He nodded to her, and they continued eating and chatting for the rest of the lunch hour.

Abby learned George was seventy years old and had worked in the store since he finished school. He knew the merchandise in the store personally. He oversaw all the new shipments they received. Jefferson's father had given him quite a lot of responsibility as he got older. He told her he loved working with the antiques.

She did detect some sadness in his voice. She did not want to get too personal, but hoped she was not the cause of his unhappiness. "George. I do not want to overstep, but are you all right with me working here? I feel you are upset about something, and I would hate to think it is because of my presence."

George put down his sandwich and smiled at Abby. "Miss, I am glad to have you in the shop. I think Mr. John would have taken to you even faster than his son has. My mood has nothing to do with you and I am sorry if I gave you that impression." He did not explain further, and Abby decided not to ask any more questions.

The remainder of the day passed by quickly. Abby again was surprised when it was time to close the shop. She followed George out of the door, and they watched as Jefferson locked up. He turned to her and nodded. "Have a good evening, Miss Abby." She told him the same and watched him walk to his car.

Jefferson walked over to her, and they walked together towards the parking lot. "Is everything all right?" he asked. Abby nodded. She was not sure if she should mention her concern about George. "Yes. I am enjoying my time in the shop so much. I feel like I have really found my passion after many years. I am a little worried about George. He is such a nice man, but he does seem sad sometimes. I did ask him if it was because of me, and he reassured me it was not."

Jefferson stopped walking and turned towards her. "George has been a part of the shop for longer than I have been alive. He watched me grow up and was a close friend and employee to our family. When my father got ill and later passed away, George felt the loss more than I did. Since I had been away travelling so much, I had not spent much of the last few years with my father. He does think you are the right fit for our shop, however. He knows that he will have to start considering slowing down at the shop soon. I am afraid that will not be easy for him. I have not said anything to him, but he understands when the shop is sold, he might have to retire."

Abby thought about Jefferson's words. "Oh no Jefferson. Please let him know if I am the new owner, his job is secure for as long as he feels he wants to remain. His knowledge of all the items in the store is invaluable. I could not manage without him."

Jefferson smiled at her response. "I am so glad to hear you say that. The next time you share lunch with him, you could mention the same thing. That should put his mind at ease."

Abby agreed and they said good night. Jefferson stood and waited until she drove out of the lot. "That is one lovely woman. Inside and outside." He thought as he drove home.

Jefferson spent his evening as he usually did. Listening to music while eating his dinner. He enjoyed sitting in the den near the fireplace. This was his father's favorite room in the entire house. His thoughts were on the shop and more so of Abby. She seemed to fit into the shop even better than he had hoped. He knew from what she had said this was the first real job she had held since her children were born.

Her comments about her late husband did make Jefferson wonder about her earlier life. She always seemed sad when she spoke of him. Jefferson had the impression what he observed was not entirely brought on from the grief over his death.

He could remember his father making comments about the possibility of him finding a wife and settling down. His father had always wanted grandchildren and Jefferson regretted never being able to give him that pleasure before he died.

He picked up the book he had been reading and tried to concentrate. His thoughts of Abby seemed to keep getting in his way. He found he had a new appreciation of getting to the shop now. Was it the fact the shop would soon change ownership. Or was it just because he could see Abby another day?

CHAPTER SEVEN:

The next few weeks went by rapidly. Abby and George started to become friends as they worked together in the shop. She was so impressed every day with his knowledge of all the antiques. He had a story about each piece of furniture. The customers always enjoyed hearing about the history of different pieces. It helped to make the sale when the customer had a story to relate about their purchase.

Abby and Jefferson spent time together several times during the week for lunch at the café. She found he was very smart and had many remarkable stories about his travels abroad. She told him she had never travelled further than Boston, so his stories were always interesting to her.

She wondered if his fondness for travelling had kept him from having any close relationships in his life. He had such a warm and friendly personality. She found it hard to believe there was not a woman in his life. Their conversations usually skirted around anything too personal. She tried to keep her questions professional, but it did not keep her curiosity from wondering about his personal life.

Abby was surprised to see her month was at an end. Jefferson had not mentioned anything to her about the financial aspects of buying the antique shop. She only hoped she would be able to acquire a loan if necessary.

Jefferson came over to her towards the end of the day and asked her to come with him to dinner after they closed the shop. She accepted his invitation with hopes this was the meeting about whether he thought she was a suitable buyer.

George and Abby walked out and waited until Jefferson had locked the door. George said good night and walked to the parking lot. Jefferson turned to Abby, "Do you need to go home? If not, you could ride with me to the restaurant." She told him that sounded like a good idea. She tried to think of some casual conversation while they drove out of town.

When they arrived at a small inn a few miles outside of Cobble Bay, Jefferson pulled into the parking lot. "Have you ever eaten here?" he asked. Abby said she did not think so. "It looks very quaint." He smiled and told her that is why he chose it. "I thought you might enjoy the décor and the food is exceptional."

Abby was pleasantly surprised when they walked inside. The Inn was small on the outside, but inside it opened into a large space. There was a huge stone fireplace in the dining room. Several small tables surrounded the area. There were some people seated at the tables, but it was not overcrowded.

The host showed them to a quiet table in the corner not too far from the fireplace. Jefferson gave their drink orders and they sat quietly for a few minutes. Abby looked around at the paintings and observed some other displays of early family crests. She told him that it appeared they had stepped back in time with the furniture and memorabilia on the walls.

Jefferson laughed and agreed with her comment. "Yes. It does. My father and mother would bring me here on special occasions when I was a child. I had to be on my best behavior. They had a few suits of armor in the entryway at that time. I always wanted to sneak away and inspect them closer, but my father would not allow it."

After the waiter brought their wine and their salads, Jefferson looked over at Abby. "I know you are probably wondering why I invited you to dinner." She nodded. "I am hoping it is to discuss the sale of the shop." Jefferson smiled and did not comment for a few minutes.

"I have observed you during the last few weeks. You have the ability to run the antique shop. More importantly, you have shown me how important the shop has become to you. You seem to care about the items going to just the right people. My father always felt that way. He would size up a customer and almost immediately know what they were looking for. He could tell whether they were a serious buyer or just browsing to waste some time. I have seen you show that same intuition."

Abby listened and did not comment. Finally, she asked if he had made a definite decision. He smiled and nodded in response to her inquiry. "Yes, Abby. I am positive you are the perfect person that my father would approve of to purchase his shop." She felt so relieved that she wanted to jump up and kiss him right in the middle of the restaurant. Of course, she restrained herself.

Jefferson laughed at her response. "You look like the child who just received all his gifts from his wish list at Christmas." She laughed and said that was the perfect explanation of her feelings.

CHAPTER EIGHT:

Abby and Jefferson sat enjoying their meal. She was not sure how to bring up the matter of purchase price. When they were finished and coffee had been brought to the table, she found her nerve.

"Now that you have decided, we need to discuss the financial side of the sale. I do have enough for a sizeable purchase, but I might need to obtain a small business loan for any additional funds."

Jefferson saw her face and knew he was about to totally amaze her. He had left the best news for the end of their dinner. "Abby, I told you my father approved of selling, but with certain reservations." She saw how serious he looked and started to worry that the price was too high for her even with additional loans.

He continued, "my father wished for someone to own the shop that loved it as much as he did. He was not concerned about how much money exchanged hands." Abby listened and started to become confused.

Jefferson reached in his jacket pocket and pulled out a legal looking paper. He handed it to Abby. He sat and watched as she read the copy of his father's will. Her look of worry started to change in front of his eyes. She stopped reading and looked up at him. "Jefferson. I do not understand. Am I reading this correctly? Your father is bequeathing the shop to whoever you determine to be the perfect fit? He is giving the shop away to a perfect stranger? "Jefferson smiled and started to laugh. "Yes, Abby. That is exactly what my father is doing. You should see your face. It is precious."

Abby sat speechless for quite some time. How could this be? Why would someone give something away that meant so much to them. Especially something of such terrific value. She looked at Jefferson and could not stop the tears that started to run down her cheeks.

Jefferson became concerned when he saw Abby's reaction to his father's wishes. "Please do not get upset. My father knew exactly what he was doing when he drafted this will." She looked at him and tried to regain her composure. "Are you certain the shop should not remain in your family's possession?"

Jefferson told her he intended to honor his father's wishes. He told her he would contact his attorney and have the proper paperwork available for her signature by the next day. "I will remain at the shop for another few weeks to help you with any questions. I know you spoke to George about staying on and he was incredibly pleased with your decision. He will be a major help to you in the coming months."

They completed their business and after Jefferson paid their bill, he walked her out of the restaurant to his car. The drive back to town was quiet. Jefferson hoped she had calmed down from the initial shock about her acquiring the shop. He was pleased to be staying on at the shop for a few weeks. His intentions were not only to be of assistance during the ownership transition. He wanted to get to know Abby better personally.

He stood and watched as she drove her car away from the lot. "Father, you have made that lovely woman incredibly happy with your strange request. I am certain she will live up to our expectations."

CHAPTER NINE:

Abby had trouble falling asleep that night. All she could think about was the news Jefferson had given her about his father's will. She found it to be the most amazing thing she had ever heard.

She was even more anxious to see her children and explain about her new venture. She knew they would be as shocked as she had been. They would be arriving on Friday for a weekend visit, and it seemed like she had not seen them for such a long time.

The next day at the shop she walked in to find a large bouquet of flowers in the office. George and Jefferson were there early waiting for her to arrive. They had a box of fresh pastries from the bakery and coffee. George congratulated her on the good news. She saw his name as well as Jefferson's on the flower arrangement.

George took the bank deposit across the street while she sat in the office with Jefferson. "Thank you again Jefferson. I was wondering if you were available on Saturday to come for dinner. My family will be in town for the weekend, and I would love for you to meet them."

He told her that he would be honored to meet her children. He did not let her know that this would help with his plan to get better acquainted with her.

The day proceeded as usual. The customer traffic had increased with the weekend closer. Jefferson joined them in the shop to assist with the customers throughout the afternoon. When closing time came finally, the three were all exhausted.

Jefferson told George and Abby to go home while he finished the bank deposit. He said he would drop it at the bank on his way home since it was Friday. The day had been very profitable, and he did not want to leave the money in the store over the weekend.

Abby gave him directions to her house and told him dinner would be at seven on Saturday. She told George to have a good weekend and walked to her car carrying the flowers they had given her.

Jefferson sat in the quiet shop and finished his paperwork. He started thinking about Abby. He knew she was some years older than he was, but that really did not matter to him. He had become very fond of her during the last month. He found her quite intelligent and was attracted to her pleasant personality.

He was not aware of any relationships she may be involved with. All he knew was that he wanted to get closer to Abby. Now that their business dealings were settled, he decided it was time to concentrate on her personally.

It had been quite some time since he had any female companionship. The day-to-day closeness they had shared made him start to think that Abby may be someone to fill that loneliness he felt in his life.

Abby was pleased to see her son's car in her driveway when she arrived. He was standing near the porch helping his little son build a snowman. He waved as she parked her car and watched as her grandson raced to meet his grandmother. "Nana, Nana." Abby laughed as she opened the door and little Hank dove into her arms.

The three walked up the stairs together as her daughter-in-law opened the front door. "Alice. So great to see you all." They followed Abby inside and she helped Hank off with his jacket.

I cannot believe how much you have grown Hank. He smiled up at her and hugged her legs. They walked into the den and Abby was pleased to see her granddaughter smiling as she rocked in her swing near the fireplace. "Oh. She is more beautiful than I remembered." Abby walked over and gave the baby girl a kiss on the forehead.

Henry grabbed his mother for a hug. "It is so good to see you, Mom. How are you?" Alice watched her as she sat down next to Hank. "You are glowing Mother. What is your secret?"

Abby just smiled and laughed at the question. If they only knew, she thought. "I am just so pleased to see you all." She told them that Cassie and Jake should be arriving soon. "I got a text from her just before I got home."

They sat for a brief time catching up on the news. Abby heard a car horn and knew Cassie had arrived. She did not know if they had shared their news with Henry, so she said nothing.

Cassie came rushing in the door followed by Jake carrying their bags. "Hi everyone. Hope we are not late." she said smiling. Jake waved and placed the bags in the hall near the stairs. Cassie ran over and hugged Abby followed by her husband.

Henry gave his sister a hug and noticed how radiant she looked. "Wow, another one who looks like the cat that ate the canary." Cassie laughed and looked at Jake. "I don't have the slightest idea what you are talking about." She reached down to give her nephew a big hug as he ran to her. "You are becoming such a little man. Are you taking care of your baby sister?" He smiled and shook his head. "Yup." he answered.

CHAPTER TEN:

Everyone sat around the room relaxing from their trip home. Abby looked at all their faces and felt such warmth in her heart for her family. She had seen them two months before when Annie had been born, but it seemed like so much longer.

"What are the plans for dinner?" Henry asked. "I am famished." Abby laughed. "The same Henry I see. Your stomach has not changed since you were a boy like your son." She told them she had food cooking in the crockpot, and they would eat as soon as she could set the table.

Alice stood and followed her to the kitchen. Cassie tagged along behind them. She grabbed Abby's hand and pulled her aside. "You didn't say anything did you Mom?" Abby just shook her head no and proceeded to get the dishes out of the cabinet.

Alice had noticed the whispering but said nothing. It only took them a few minutes to set the table. The girls finished while Abby took the food from the crockpot and placed it in a bowl for the table. She had fresh rolls to go with the stew she had prepared earlier before work.

Henry and Jake walked into the kitchen followed by Hank. Once they were all seated, Abby pulled out a bottle of wine and placed it on the table. She watched as everyone got seated before offering a toast to the family. "Thank you, God, for bringing my family home safely." They all raised their glasses and joined in Abby's toast.

The stew was passed around with the warm rolls. "Looks great Mom. I miss your tasty stew." said Henry as he took a large serving. Alice put some in a small bowl for Hank. She had a bowl in front of her and tried to manage holding baby Annie while she ate.

Abby offered to take the baby from Alice. "It is ok Mother. I am used to juggling my food and Annie at the same time." She watched as Hank seemed to like the stew as much as his father did.

They all sat eating and chatting about the family news. When they had all finished and sat back relaxing, Cassie stood. "Now that we all are done eating, I have an announcement." She looked over at her husband who was grinning broadly.

Henry looked at his sister and then at her husband. "Oh brother. Am I going to be an uncle finally?" Cassie shook her head. "Boy, you always have to jump the gun bro." They all laughed, and Alice jumped up to grab Cassie. The hugs and congratulations lasted for a while. Abby just sat watching her noisy family enjoying the news.

She stood once everyone had calmed down. She thought to herself that she hoped they would be as excited and happy about her news. "Well, now that you all have heard the wonderful news from Cassie and Jake, I also have some news to share with you all."

They stopped talking and listened to Abby. "You are not pregnant too, are you Mom?" Henry said as everyone laughed. Abby smiled. "No, smarty. However, my news is just as exciting to me. She hesitated a few minutes. "I have begun a new chapter in my life. I am now the proud owner of an antique store in town."

Her family sat without saying a word. They just looked at Abby and then at each other. Finally, Cassie spoke. "Mom? What are you talking about? Why would you purchase a shop? Who will run it?" Abby smiled. "Well, because I chose to, and I will run it of course."

CHAPTER ELEVEN:

Abby sat down and watched as her family remained quiet. She expected the news to be surprising to the family. She did not expect the concerned faces she saw before her.

Henry finally broke the silence. "Mom. Are you being serious with us? You really own an antique shop in Cobble Bay?" Abby nodded in response unable to find the right words to explain her decision. He started to speak again when Alice touched his arm. He stopped and turned to his wife. "Your mother wants to have a new career and I think it is wonderful." she said.

When the others heard Alice's comment, they all realized what she said was true. They had always thought of their mother being at home. They never gave it much thought that her life might be missing something. Cassie walked over to her mother and gave her a hug. "If this is really something you are excited about then we are too."

Henry took his sister's cue and followed with a hug and words of encouragement. He did add that he hoped the investment was a sound one for her budget. Abby smiled at him. "Yes Henry. The investment is not much for me at all. I just must show up every day and take care of the customers that arrive."

They listened to her as she explained about the location of the store. She told them about working there during the recent month and how much she enjoyed her days. She told them about George and his knowledge and dedication to the shop. She also told them about Jefferson. She said they would meet him on Saturday when he joined them for dinner.

When they had all calmed down, she explained about the will and how she had become the new owner of Cobble's Antique Emporium.

They sat in silence again trying to understand how the shop had become hers. Henry looked at her. "You are serious. The shop was just given to you. No investment? No strings attached?"

Abby nodded at her son's questions. "I understand your disbelief. I felt the same when Jefferson showed me his father's will. I was prepared with the funds that your father left to me. I may still use some of the money to freshen the shop up a little bit. I cannot wait for you all to see it. I fell in love with the shop during my weeks working there. After being at home for so long, I had no idea what I needed in my life. Once I started going to the shop every day, it was exactly what I needed to have purpose in my life."

They all reassured her that they all still needed her in their lives. Abby smiled at their responses. "Yes, I know you do. I need all of you too. But this is something else. I feel the shop has filled the space that I have felt in my life for such a long time. Even before your father passed away. He had the hospital. Once you all were grown and making your own lives, I felt so alone at times. Now, I am so happy every day. I cannot wait to get to the shop every morning and I hate to leave when it is time to close the doors."

Henry commented that it was great to see her so excited about this new venture. He did still have his doubts, but he kept them to himself as he watched his mother beaming with happiness.

CHAPTER TWELVE:

The evening ended early. Abby remained downstairs enjoying her wine by the fireplace. She knew her children were happy for her. She also knew they were concerned about her decision. Once they meet Jefferson and realize this is really happening, hopefully they will feel more at ease," she thought.

After Alice got Hank settled in for the night, she climbed into bed alongside her husband. "What are you thinking?" she asked him. Henry smiled at her and pulled her close to him. "Nothing," he answered. Alice smiled. "I know you better than that Henry. I can see the doubt and worry all over your face. You do realize your mother is a very smart and confident person. I know she did not make this decision easily. Just allow her some credit. It is going to be the best thing for her right now. She needs purpose in her life other than being a mother and grandmother. Give it some time."

He listened and nodded. Thinking to himself that his wife was correct with her description of Abby. He was not going to judge whether she was right or wrong. He would, however, be watching in case this venture started to go south. He leaned over and kissed Alice. She closed her eyes, and they were both asleep faster than they expected.

The next day started early with baby Annie crying. Abby woke confused for a moment with the sound. Then she smiled when she remembered the house was full of her family. She got up and put on her robe. When she got down to the kitchen, Alice was already at the kitchen table nursing the baby.

"Such a beautiful sight first thing in the morning," she remarked. Alice smiled and Abby noticed the look of contentment on her face. "I used to love these early morning feedings with Henry and Cassie. The house was quiet, and I could just concentrate on their little faces. It was my time of complete peace and enjoyment before the day began."

Alice listened to her and noticed a look of sadness that came over Abby's face. "Mother? I can say this without Henry around. You and his father did not share the same feelings about him and his sister. Did you?" Abby was surprised at Alice's comment. She did not answer, but just shook her head no.

Before anything else could be said, Henry came bounding down the stairs chasing his little son. "Nana, Nana. It snowed more last night. Can we play outside Daddy?" Henry scooped his son up in his arms and told him they could if he ate all his breakfast first.

Abby took that as her cue and went to the pantry to get the pancake mix. "How about chocolate chip pancakes?" Hank squirmed out of his father's arms. "Oh boy." he responded to Abby's remark. He stood by her side and watched as she mixed the pancakes. She let him add the chocolate chips.

Henry pulled out the tin of coffee and filled the measuring cup. Abby smiled and watched as he prepared the pot of coffee. He pulled out the milk and poured a glass for Hank. "How about you sit by Mama and drink your milk while your pancakes are cooking." Hank did as his father suggested without an argument.

He watched as his baby sister nursed from his mother. He looked at Alice and smiled. "Did I eat my breakfast that way when I was a baby?" he asked. Alice nodded and told her young son that he had enjoyed his meals from her for quite some time. She waited for some additional questions, but Hank just drank his milk.

Abby walked over to the table and placed a plate with pancakes, topped with whip cream and more chocolate chips in front of Hank. He looked at the plate and then up at his grandmother. Without any comment, he started gobbling up the food in front of him.

"Whoa there kiddo. Slow down. The snow will wait until you get outside. Eat slower or you will have a tummy ache." Abby told him. She was glad he enjoyed the treat in front of him. He listened to her words and took his time chewing and eating slower. "OK Nana."

Abby returned to the stove and cooked additional pancakes for the others. She also prepared a pan of sausage links and strips of bacon. She knew Cassie and Jake would be down soon, so she wanted to be prepared.

Henry helped himself to some pancakes and bacon before she placed them in the oven to keep warm until the others came downstairs. She just shook her head as she watched her son start eating as fast as little Hank. "Do I have to tell you about a possible tummy ache too?" she asked him.

Hank looked at his father and started to laugh. "Daddy will get an ache in his tummy too. Right Nana?" She nodded and they all started laughing at Hank's comments.

Jake walked into the kitchen. "What is so funny?" Hank told him about Nana telling his father to eat slower before his tummy ached.

Jake sat down after getting a cup of coffee. He told Hank that was good advice. "Where is Cassie? Sleeping in?" Abby asked.

Jake shook his head no. "She will be down in a while. Had to take care of something in the bathroom first." They all understood his meaning. Abby thought, "morning sickness." she remembered the feeling. Hers had not only been mornings but with Henry it lasted off and on all day for the first few months. Then she felt better than she ever had for the remainder of her pregnancy.

Abby brought the pancakes to the table along with the plate of meat. She had just taken a bite when Cassie came down the stairs. She still glowed but was just slightly green around the edges. "Would you like a cup of tea dear? It might help to settle your stomach." Cassie thanked her mother and sat down at the table next to Jake.

"How did everyone sleep last night?" Abby asked. They all said they had no problems. "Between the long drive, the great meal and the wine, I think we all slept like babies." remarked Henry.

Hank finished all the pancakes on his plate and asked if he could go out and play in the snow. "Well, we have to get you bundled up first," answered Alice. Henry followed his wife's suggestion and stood up from the table. He took Hank's plate and his to the sink. Finishing the last of his coffee he followed Hank up the stairs to get dressed for their excursion outside in the cold and new snowfall.

Alice followed shortly with baby Annie. When Abby was alone with Cassie and Jake, she asked them what they thought about her news. "I know your brother has his reservations, but I would like you to be truthful. Do you think I am crazy too?"

Jake looked at his wife and spoke. "No, we do not mother. Yes, it did sound strange when you explained about the will, but just by seeing your enthusiasm we think it is great. We cannot wait to see the shop for ourselves. Is it open today?"

Abby told them the shop was closed for the weekend. She planned to ask Jefferson for the keys when he arrived later for dinner. That way they could see the shop before they left for home on Sunday. Cassie agreed with her husband's comments. "I am incredibly happy for you Mom. Jake is right. You seem so excited that we cannot be anything but thrilled for your new adventure."

Once breakfast was done, Cassie helped clear the dishes and put them in the dishwasher. She said she was going upstairs to take a shower. Jake followed behind her leaving Abby alone in the kitchen. She watched out the window as her son and grandson were trying to build another snowman in the new coating of snow.

The ringing of the phone startled her. She was surprised to hear Jefferson when she answered. "Good morning, Abby. I hope I am not calling at an inconvenient time. I was wondering if you had told your family about the shop." She told him she had the night before. "I think they are trying to be supportive of their crazy mother." she told him. "Do you think it would help if they saw the shop?" he asked her. "I plan to go there later today and thought you could all meet up with me. I have the paperwork for you to sign and we can make it official."

Abby smiled and told him that would be wonderful. She told him they would meet him there sometime after noon. He agreed and said he would see her then. She stood holding the phone when Alice came downstairs. "Everything ok Mother?" she asked.

Abby told her about Jefferson's call. Alice agreed they were all anxious to see the shop. "I think it will make us all feel better," Alice replied. She pulled on her coat and joined Henry and Hank outside in the yard. Abby watched as she spoke to Henry. He nodded and looked toward the back door. Waving to his mother, he took a direct hit of a snowball thrown by his wife. Abby watched as he ran after his wife. Hank joined in the fun and soon they were all tossing snowballs at each other.

Abby went upstairs to shower and dress for the day. She had always dressed in suits for the shop but decided on jeans and a sweater today. It was Saturday and the shop was officially closed.

She stopped in the hall near Cassie's room. She tapped lightly and Jake answered the door. She could see Cassie laying on top of the quilt sound asleep. He walked out into the hall. She told him about the plans for the afternoon and he agreed they were also anxious to visit the shop.

She left him as he watched over his sleeping wife. Grabbing her coat, she went outside to join the rest of the family. When Hank saw her, he grabbed a snowball from his father and ran to her. His aim was not the best and it missed completely. She laughed and pretended to chase him around the garden with her own snowball.

CHAPTER THIRTEEN:

When the group came inside to get warm, they found Cassie and Jake sitting in the den by the fire. They all asked Cassie how she was feeling. She told them her stomach had calmed down thanks to the tea and crackers her mother had fixed earlier.

Abby went to the kitchen to make everyone some hot cocoa. She loved being outside with her little grandson. Hank was such a joy. She could not wait for Annie to get old enough to play with them. When she carried the tray into the den, everyone looked pleased.

"Mom, you always know exactly what we want. It was that way when we were children. In case I have not told you recently. Thank you for always being there for us. I love you, Mom." Abby felt tears after hearing Henry's words.

Cassie said she felt the same way. "I only hope I can be as good a mother as you have always been to us," she added. Abby sat down with her mug of cocoa. "Those were the happiest days of my life. Taking care of you and teaching you both when you were toddlers. They were the most meaningful moments in my life."

Henry looked at Abby. "Yes, and now you will start on making new special moments." She smiled and told him that being a grandmother did have its own rewards. "Oh, I know that. I was referring to the antique shop this time. It should provide you with many new accomplishments and pleasure."

Abby agreed with him. They sat chatting and enjoying the hot cocoa. Hank sat next to Abby on the sofa. "What are we going to do after we finish our cocoa?" he asked.

"Well Hank. We are going for a drive into town to look at Grandma's new store." Hank looked at his father for a moment. He looked back at Abby. "You have a store? Are there any toys in the store?" She laughed and gave her grandson a big hug. "I am not sure Hank. But I bet we could look around for some." "Yea," he responded.

After they were done Abby took the cups to the kitchen on the tray. The others got ready for their drive to town. Abby decided to ride with Cassie since there was more room with no children's car seats.

As they all parked in front of the shop, Abby watched her children's faces to see their reaction. They all seemed curious as they walked up to the door. Abby knocked quietly on the glass. She saw Jefferson walking towards them. He unlocked and opened the door telling everyone welcome. "Please come in." he told the crowd.

Abby stood back and watched her family enter the shop. Hank started to ask questions as soon as he walked through the door. His father told him to be patient and wait a few minutes. Abby closed the door and introduced Jefferson to her family.

Henry reached out to shake hands first. Jake followed the same gesture. "We are very pleased to meet you sir." Henry said. "This is a very nice shop you have here." Jefferson smiled and thanked him for his comment. "Yes, it has been in my family for quite some time. I started coming here when I was around this young man's age." He said looking at Hank.

After all the introductions were made, Jefferson asked Abby to join him in his office while the group spread out looking around the store. Once inside, he took a paper from his desk and handed it to Abby.

While he looked for his pen, he explained the document was exactly what he had told her about the ownership of the shop.

Abby read it over and saw there were no strange additions. It simply said the shop was hers, free and clear, according to the terms of John Sampson's last will. She was the full and only owner of the shop. The Sampson family would hold no further claim to anything pertaining to the profits made in the shop. Jefferson Sampson would be available to advise her on any questions pertaining to the daily business. It also stated that George would remain as their head clerk in the store until he decided to retire.

Abby took the pen from Jefferson and signed the documents. One for her and another for Jefferson. When she reached over to take the keys from Jefferson a hearty cheer rose from the crowd standing behind them. She turned to see her entire family clapping and cheering for her.

Jefferson started to laugh when he saw her children's reaction. "I am pleased to see you all support your mother's new endeavor. I am sure that means a lot to her."

Abby laughed amidst the cheers and hugs that followed the signing. She was sure her children had no idea just how proud she was at that very moment.

CHAPTER FOURTEEN:

Abby walked around the shop followed by her family. She pointed out different pieces of furniture that were particularly interesting. Hank was disappointed that he did not find any toys in the shop. He began to get upset when Jefferson walked up to him with a small metal truck in his hand. "I thought you would like to take this truck home with you. I really enjoyed playing with it when I was a boy. It has been lonely because there are no boys to keep it company any longer." Hank looked at him and then looked at his father. "Can I have the truck, Daddy?" Henry nodded and told him to be sure to thank Jefferson for the gift. Hank took the truck from Jefferson and did as his father suggested. He then walked over to a spot on the floor near the office and sat down inspecting the truck very carefully.

"Looks like you just made a friend for life." Abby told Jefferson. Henry walked over to him. "Was that really one of your toys?" he asked. Jefferson nodded. "It might be worth something as an antique toy. Are you certain you do not want to keep it, even for sentimental value?" Jefferson assured him that he was glad to give the truck to someone who would obviously love it like he had.

The group spent the next hour looking over everything. Jefferson stood back and made himself available if they had any questions. He told Henry the upstairs was used to hold extra inventory. There was also a basement, but it was too damp to keep any valuable pieces for too long. Henry asked if he could look upstairs, and Jefferson walked him over to the door and turned on the lights for him.

Abby had been upstairs a few times with George. She knew briefly what items were in storage. Henry came down after some time. "There are a few trunks up there that look interesting. Do you have keys for them?" he asked Jefferson. He told Henry he had keys for one of them. He also told him it held old books that would be put out on the shelves when they had room.

"The other trunk has a very distinctly shaped key. I have looked through my father's desk and have not found it. It was left here years ago by a sailor who worked on one of our fishing boats. The man died in an accident shortly after and no one ever came to claim the trunk."

Henry looked at Abby. "That sounds like a mystery to me Mother. Too bad I must return home. I would love to investigate that further." Jefferson told him that he had tried to locate family members of the sailor but found none. The young man was not a native of Cobble Bay so none of the residents could help with his inquiries.

"If the key is ever located, I sure would like to be around when you open it." Henry told Abby. She smiled and told Jefferson, Henry was a businessman by day and Indiana Jones at night. Jefferson and the rest of the group laughed at Abby's description of her son.

After a few hours, they decided it was time to leave so Jefferson could return to his home. "We will see you later for dinner," Henry told him as they walked outside. Jefferson told Abby he was looking forward to getting further acquainted with her family.

She walked out feeling pleased with herself over her newly acquired shop. She hoped she did not let anyone down when she started running the business.

CHAPTER FIFTEEN:

The dinner proved to be an enormous success. Jefferson arrived right on time carrying two bottles of wine. Abby welcomed him inside and he noticed Hank playing with the truck he had given him. "Well, looks like the little guy hasn't gotten tired of that truck so far."

Henry shook his hand and invited him to join the others in the den. Jefferson looked around the room when he entered. "This is a nice room. I love the shelves of books around the fireplace. Looks extremely comfortable. Good place to curl up and read." Abby agreed and told him she spent many hours doing exactly that.

She walked back to the kitchen to check on the meal. Alice and Cassie were setting the table in the dining room. "He seems like a very nice man mother," they said to Abby. She nodded. "Yes, he has been so helpful. He was very patient with me when I was first working in the shop. I still cannot believe the shop is mine." They both hugged her and said how proud they were of her.

The girls helped set out the dinner and Abby went to the den to let the men know everything was ready. She showed Jefferson a place at the table and after everyone was seated, he made sure they all had some wine. "I would like to toast Abigail and wish her the best of luck with the antique shop." They all joined in and wished their mother many years of happiness with her new business.

The children were all on their best behavior with Jefferson. Henry did not show any signs of being concerned about Abby's decision. He spent most of the evening listening to Jefferson speak of the early days he spent in the shop with his father.

Jefferson managed to win over all the family, Abby noticed. He was pleasant and listened to them discuss their lives. He learned what a devoted mother Abby had been when they were growing up. He heard how their father had been too busy with the hospital to be able to spend much time at home with them.

He watched Abby as she listened to her children. He could see the pride she had in all of them. Cassie and Jake were both beaming with the news about their impending addition. He could not help but think what a young grandmother she was.

Alice turned to Jefferson and asked if he had ever thought about settling down with a wife and children. He told her it had not fit into his traveling schedule. "Now that I am older, I just might consider it. By the look of your family, it does have a certain appeal." She smiled and glanced over at Abby.

"Would you ever want to remarry mother?" Abby was shocked by her question. "Where did that come from? I am incredibly happy and content with my life. Now with the shop to fill my days, I think my life will be quite complete thank you."

They all laughed, and Henry did not comment further about his wife's inquiry. He waited until later when they were in bed to comment. "Why did you ask my mother about getting married again?" Alice just smiled. "I just thought there might be some attraction between her and Jefferson. Did you notice how he was watching her during dinner? I think he would like to get better acquainted with her."

Henry did not answer her. He had noticed how attentive Jefferson had been to Abby. He seemed like a nice enough man. However, he did not think of him as a romantic interest to his mother. Of course, he had never really thought about her finding anyone to take his father's place. He agreed it might be possible someday, but someone who was so much younger. That did make him uncomfortable.

The next day the family packed up to drive back to their homes. Abby had enjoyed having them all visit and did not like to say goodbye to any of them. She walked outside as they put their luggage into their vehicles. She stood next to Cassie hugging her and not wanting to let her leave. "I am so happy for you and Jake. Please keep in touch and let me know how everything is progressing.

"I will mom. Do not worry about me. I am sure this morning sickness will be gone soon. I plan to enjoy every moment of this pregnancy. I am loving all the extra attention from Jake." Abby laughed. She had a flashback to her pregnancy with Henry. Joseph was not pleased when he was told. He tried to be attentive, but his mind was always on the hospital and his duties there. He always made her realize the family held second place to his career. "I know Jake will take loving care of you." She kissed her daughter and waved as they drove away.

Henry came over and gave her a kiss on the cheek. "Mother. Stay safe and not too busy at the shop. We are immensely proud of you. I cannot wait to hear how everything works out." As he got into the car he yelled back to her, "let me know if you find that key." Abby shook her head and waved to them all. She saw Hank blowing kisses to her from his car seat. She blew some back to him and laughed.

As she watched her children drive away a feeling of loneliness came over her. When she walked into the house the phone was ringing. She answered to hear Jefferson's voice. "Hello Abby. I thought you might be feeling sad with the children leaving. How would you like to have dinner with me. We could discuss the shop or just enjoy each other's company for a while."

She was surprised at the invitation but thought it would help to get her mind off the big empty house. "That sounds wonderful." He said he would pick her up at seven. "Dress casual and comfortable," he added before he hung up the phone.

Abby went inside and busied herself with changing the bedding in the guest rooms. She fixed a light lunch and went to the den to read until it was time to dress for dinner.

Jefferson pulled in the drive shortly before seven. Abby had decided on slacks and a sweater. She felt like she had dressed too casually, until she saw Jefferson at the door. He was wearing jeans and a sweater. She opened the door and he waited while she grabbed her coat. He opened the car door for her and when she was seated, he walked around to the driver side. Well, a gentleman. What a pleasant change from most of the men she saw lately.

He drove out to the country and pulled into a little inn that she had seen a few times. When they walked inside, there was only a small amount of people in the dining room. They were seated by the windows that overlooked a pretty patio.

"I would have asked to sit outside, but the weather really is not warm enough. I do not mind the cooler temperatures, but not when I am trying to enjoy a delicious meal." She nodded in agreement.

Jefferson ordered a bottle of wine and after the host had served their drinks, they sat talking while they waited for their dinners to arrive.

"I enjoyed meeting your family, Abby. They all seem to care about your welfare. That is refreshing to witness. Some young people today feel they are the center of the universe and care less about their parents.

"My children have always made me proud. They never let their feelings interfere with always striving to reach their goals. Joseph was not the most affectionate person with me or them. I tried to make up for what they did not receive from him. That is why his death did not hit them so hard. They had already gotten used to him not being a part of their lives long before he passed away."

The evening was spent talking about the shop. Jefferson explained more details to her about the daily paperwork she would have to do as the owner. He was impressed with her excitement about running the shop.

Abby was surprised when she noticed the time. The time had gone by so fast. She found she enjoyed spending time with Jefferson outside of the shop. He was quite interesting, and she enjoyed listening to his stories about his travels.

The drive back to her house was quiet. She wondered if it would be a good idea to invite him inside for coffee. Before she had a chance to decide, he had pulled into the driveway. He walked her up to the porch and started to tell her good night.

She decided it would be best to keep their relationship on a business level and did not ask about the coffee. After he drove away, she went upstairs after checking the doors and turning out the lights.

She was looking forward to the next day and her first step in becoming the owner of the Cobble Bay Antique Emporium. She hoped it would be the great adventure she hoped for.

CHAPTER SIXTEEN:

Jefferson arrived at the shop the next day and noticed Abby's car already parked near the entrance. He smiled to himself and walked in to find her hard at work rearranging some of the front window displays.

"Good morning boss," he said. She laughed and continued her work. "Hello yourself Jefferson. I thought I would freshen up the displays. I hope you do not mind." He told her it was her shop, and she could change anything she wanted to.

They both were standing near the windows when George arrived. He told them both good morning and walked to the back to put his lunch in the refrigerator. When he came out, Abby asked him what his thoughts were about the changes to the displays. He looked at Jefferson before he answered.

"I want your honest opinion, George. It will not hurt my feelings if you think anything should be changed. He smiled at her. "Well, Miss Abby. I have thought for some time that we really needed to change those windows around." Jefferson looked at him and started to laugh. "Why didn't you ever suggest that to me George?" he asked.

George told him that his father had overseen the displays and made it quite clear that he controlled any changes that were made. "I just assumed you felt the same, so I never said anything different about them to you."

Abby and Jefferson went back to the office and left George to his daily cleaning and straightening of merchandise. "I enjoyed dinner last night," Jefferson told her. Abby agreed and they spent the morning going over the accounting ledgers for the store. "Have you ever thought about putting the ledgers into a program on the computer?" she asked him. "It would be faster and much more efficient."

He thought about her question and decided it did sound like a good idea. She explained about the program she used at home for her daily budget with household expenses. "There is a business program that is similar. It would help with inventory. It could also be used to keep track of George's salary and taxes."

He agreed to look at the program after lunch. They spent the next few hours talking about how most of the store's inventory was acquired. Jefferson asked her to accompany him to the café for lunch and she accepted. They walked across the street while George watched from inside the shop.

He smiled as he walked to the kitchen. "Mr. John, I think your son is starting to look at our new lady as more than just the owner." He hummed to himself as he sat eating his sandwich and reading the morning paper.

Jefferson sat during lunch and listened while Abby explained further about the benefits of having their inventory on the computer. He watched as her face seemed to light up talking about the shop. He knew his father was watching and nodding his head in approval for his son's decision about the shop.

They returned after lunch to find George waiting on quite a few customers. Abby walked over to a couple who were looking at some of the newly placed items in the window. "May I be on any assistance?" she asked. They told her they had just moved into an older home in the area and were looking for some additional furniture to fill the living room.

While Abby spoke to them, Jefferson helped George with customers who had some questions about the china they had on display. The afternoon went by with quite a few more customers than usual for this part of the week.

When closing time came around, Abby was just completing a sale of a lovely chair that she had moved into the front of the store. After Jefferson locked the door, he followed her into the office. "Looks like your decision about the window displays really attracted some new business today." he told her as she sat down behind the desk. Abby smiled at his comment. "Yes, you are right about that. Strange how something so small can attract people."

George walked in behind them and said how many people commented on how different the store looked. Abby was so pleased with the response she was hearing. "I think you have a real knack for decorating." George told her. She thanked him for the compliment.

He told them good night and let himself out the back door. Jefferson turned to Abby and told her she should be incredibly pleased with herself. "I am afraid I am not used to all the flattering comments," she told him. He laughed and told her she should be ready for that to change.

He waited until she finished the receipts for the day. After she placed the bank bag in the safe, they walked outside together. Jefferson locked the front door and handed her the keys. "I may be late in the morning. I have some travel plans to look over with my agent." he said. She nodded and told him good night.

He waited until she was in her car before he entered his vehicle. He thought about her on the drive home. He was curious about her feelings for him but thought it would be too forward to ask at this early stage.

CHAPTER SEVENTEEN:

Abby pulled in her driveway tired but happy. The day had turned out to be very encouraging. Not only for her self-esteem, but profitable for the shop as well.

After fixing a light dinner, she curled up in the den with a book and a glass of wine. She found herself wondering what Jefferson's next trip would be and how soon he would leave. She valued his help with the shop. She knew the day would come when he would depart for another adventure. She just hoped it would not be soon.

She realized she enjoyed his company both in the shop and when they were dining together. He told such interesting stories about all his trips. She had never been someone who wanted to travel further than New England. After listening to Jefferson tell her about some of the exotic places he had seen, she started to think she would like to see more of the world.

Then she realized it was not the locations that she found interesting it was spending more time with Jefferson. She was surprised with the realization that she was becoming fonder of Jefferson than she anticipated.

Her life with Joseph had not been as fulfilling during the final few years. He was consumed with the bank and when he was at home with her it still seemed like his mind was elsewhere.

They rarely shared any intimate moments. It had become normal for him to give her a small kiss on the cheek when he left in the morning. Then he would do the same at night before he rolled over to his side of the bed and fell asleep almost immediately.

Abby had thought their life as spouses was so full when they first married. He was so attentive to her needs. He was so affectionate and went out of his way to please her both physically and emotionally. She always felt satisfied after their love making.

Things began to change when she told him she was pregnant. He pretended he was pleased, but she felt he was not being truthful with her. As time went on and her body started to change with the baby that was growing inside her, he seemed to withdraw from showing her attention. His excuse was that he was worried their intimacy would harm the baby.

Abby was young and accepted that explanation. However, when his actions were the same after the birth of their son Henry, she started to think there was some other explanation to his behavior.

She tried to bring up the subject with Joseph several times, but to no avail. He always made the excuse that he was tired after work. He would act attentive for a few weeks and then eventually fall back into the same routine.

After she had made a persuasive argument about his lack of affection during an especially prolonged period, Joseph took her into his arms and smiled. "You know I love you, Abby." he told her. She was startled when he continued to carry her to their bedroom and put her on the bed. Henry had been asleep for some time, so there was no chance of any interruptions.

Joseph carefully undressed her, and his caresses became more intense. He kissed her entire body and touched places that made her forget any thoughts she had about his love for her. When their bodies came together the final climax was overwhelming. She said nothing to him, but just enjoyed the feeling of total pleasure.

It was a few weeks later that she realized she was pregnant again. She went to tell him at the bank one day during lunch. She was certain he would be as thrilled as she was. However, his reaction was not what she expected. His look of surprise and then anger took her completely by surprise. "I thought you would be pleased," she said.

He looked at her, "well you thought wrong." Abby was even more shocked when he asked if she really wanted another baby. "What are you suggesting?" she asked him. "Well. Our son is getting old enough that we can afford to do other things. I just thought a new baby would only be a sacrifice for you." Abby could not bring herself to answer him. She left his office and managed to get to her car before she broke down in tears.

She could not believe her husband who had loved her so deeply could suggest that she terminate this pregnancy. This was the turning point in their marriage. Abby was determined to love this new baby enough for both parents. She did not care about Joseph's feelings of insecurity. She would have this new baby regardless of whether their marriage would last or not.

During the first weeks of her pregnancy with Cassie, the morning sickness was terrible. She knew the stress she was feeling was not helping but she could not control her feelings about Joseph's remarks. Eventually the sickness subsided, and the pregnancy continued naturally. She did not care about the changes to her body. She would catch a glimpse of Joseph looking at her from time to time when she was dressing. His looks told her that he had not changed his mind about having another child.

When it came time for Cassie to be born, Joseph took her to the hospital after the contractions had started. Shortly after she was checked into the maternity ward Joseph announced that he had an important meeting and had to leave.

Abby was not surprised about his absence. The only embarrassment was having to explain to the nurses and her doctor. They made no comments about the absent husband, but their looks said they felt sorry for her to be alone during the birth of her baby.

When Abby heard she had a girl, she was ecstatic with joy. She loved her little boy at home, but secretly had wanted a daughter for such a long time. She realized this would be her only other pregnancy and was so pleased she now had a son and daughter to love and protect.

As she sat remembering this period in her life, she wondered how her children would feel about her getting closer to Jefferson. She had not dated since Joseph's death. She had thought it would upset them too much. Now that she was beginning to have stronger feelings about Jefferson, she decided it might be time to discuss the possibility with Henry and Cassie.

CHAPTER EIGHTEEN:

Jefferson sat in his study looking over the brochures on his desk. His travel agent had put together quite an interesting trip to Europe. The photos he saw were of beautiful landscapes and people enjoying themselves while touring the different sights. He started to daydream of seeing these places with Abby at his side. He could almost hear her laughter at seeing all the beauty that was before her.

She had told him she had not traveled far away from home. He sensed that she would love seeing these unfamiliar places and looking through the big, old castles. He knew she would love seeing all the antiques they held.

He imagined staying at some beautiful old chateau overlooking the green meadows or the snow-covered mountains in the distance. He thought about how he wanted to lay in bed alongside of her. He could picture her face as he began to caress her body. He wondered what heights he could bring her body to enjoy.

His thoughts continued for most of the evening. They managed to find their way into his dreams as well. Abby was smiling at him as they lay together. She was moaning and arching her body as his fingers fondled her breasts. He watched her as she reached for him and held him in the way he so wanted from her.

Jefferson woke in the morning not wanting to leave his bed. He tried to fall back asleep to find his dreams again, but to no avail. As he got up and walked into the shower all he could think about was Abby.

When he finally came downstairs, he went into the study. He took all the brochures and placed them in his desk drawer. "I will call my agent and tell her I am postponing any travels for the next few months. I need to concentrate on business at home right now." he thought. "My next trip will include Abby." he decided.

When Jefferson walked into the antique shop later in the day, Abby smiled at him. He saw she was assisting a customer and proceeded to the office. George came in and told him the shop had seen quite a few customers so far. "Business seems to be picking up," he announced. Jefferson nodded and went back to looking over the inventory sheets. "I heard there was an estate sale this weekend. We should check it out for any pieces we need for the shop." George waited for a response from Jefferson. Abby walked into the room just as George was telling Jefferson about the sale.

"That sounds like a wonderful idea George," she said. Jefferson looked up from the papers and nodded in agreement. "Yes, it certainly does. We have been able to find some real treasures at previous sales. People just want to clear out the old furniture. They do not realize that many others find them to be so special." He turned to Abby and asked if she would like to join him on Saturday. "We can look over the items for sale before they are sold to anyone else."

He explained the day before the actual sale was open to any dealers. They always had first choice of the inventory. She agreed to going with him on Saturday. George smiled and left the room when he saw some customers entering the shop.

"I am surprised to see you today. I thought you were going to your travel agent to review the plans for your next trip." He thought for a moment before he answered her. "Yes, that was the plan. However, when I spoke to her it turns out she did not really have anything to show me that was of interest. I told her to put off making any arrangements for a few months. This way I can be available if you have any questions about the shop. Besides, you wanted to install that new computer system for the inventory. I thought you could use my help with that. "

Abby nodded and told him that would be a good idea. That way he would know how the system worked and they could train George how to enter items when they were sold so it would update the inventory automatically. As she went out to the front of the shop, she started smiling to think Jefferson was going to be around for a while longer.

The day seemed to go by quickly with the additional customers stopping by. There were some sales and when it was time to close for lunch, she asked Jefferson if he wanted to join her at the café.

George watched as they walked out together. He hoped their friendship would continue. He had worried about Jefferson for some time. He always felt more like a father to Jefferson. Especially after John's death. When Abby first came to the shop, he thought she would make not only a good owner for the shop, but someone for Jefferson to settle down with.

George had sensed they had feelings for each other. He did not think they were aware of them yet. He had mentioned the estate sale in hopes of them going together. It looked like his plan had worked.

When Abby and Jefferson returned from lunch George was already busy with some new customers. Abby told Jefferson he should take the rest of the day off and relax. He said he did have some errands to handle and told her he would call her about their plans for Saturday.

The day ended being another profitable one for the shop. Abby settled all the receipts and after she put the deposit in the safe, she met George in the front of the shop. They closed together and he waited for her to get in her car before he headed to his vehicle.

Abby drove home thinking about meeting with Jefferson later in the week for the estate sale. She had never been to such a sale and was looking forward to finding some items for the shop.

She was eating her dinner when the phone rang. Jefferson told her he hoped he was not interrupting anything. She told him it was not a problem and they talked about the sale for quite some time. He explained how they were handled and what she could expect.

"I thought after we are through with the sale, we could take a drive into the country and have dinner somewhere. If you do not have any other plans that is." Abby agreed to his idea. She tried not to show her excitement at spending the entire day with him. She did not want him to know how much she had wanted to be with him outside the shop. "I don't want to appear too forward," she thought to herself.

For some strange reason just the thought of being with Jefferson made her feel like a teenager again. She tried not to get her hopes up about any sort of feelings he might have. "He probably would not want to date someone my age anyway." Regardless of her fears she could not keep her feelings to herself any longer.

Abby waited for her daughter to answer her call. She hoped Cassie would not be upset with her when she explained what she was feeling about Jefferson. She wanted some reassurance that she was not being a silly old lady.

CHAPTER NINETEEN:

"Hello Mom. How are you? How is the shop working out for you?" Abby told Cassie that she was fine and that the shop was becoming busier by the day. "How are you feeling? Is the morning sickness easing up some?" Cassie replied that she was starting to feel better every day.

They talked about the baby for a brief time. Finally, Abby found her nerve. "Cassie. I am calling to get your opinion on something." Her daughter was quiet while Abby explained about the feelings she was beginning to have for Jefferson. She told her she had not said anything to him. She asked her what she thought about them dating.

Cassie did not answer for a few minutes. "Mother. I am so pleased that you thought to call and ask my thoughts about you dating Jefferson or anyone. Personally, it is a wonderful idea. You have been alone far too long. Even before Dad died, I know how lonely you were. Henry and I could see that you both were unhappy. Now that Dad is gone, you need to finally make a life for yourself with someone who can love you and treat you the way you deserve."

Abby was pleased and surprised at her daughter's remarks. She never realized the children had known how unhappy their parents were with their marriage. "Oh Cassie. I am sorry that you and your brother had to witness our unhappiness. We did try to cover up our feelings, but the harder we tried the worse things got."

Cassie told her mother not to apologize. She knew how much she had tried with her father. She had seen how the affection seemed to disappear in their marriage. "I do not know what happened with Dad. He was somewhere else even when he was home with us. I know how demanding his position at the bank was. However, it did not give him a reason to pull away from you or his children. Jake and I have discussed the possibility of you finding a new love and we both agree that it would be the best thing for you.”

“What do you think your brother would say about it happening? Would he be as understanding as you?” she asked. Cassie told her it might be a little more difficult for Henry to accept. “He feels he has been the man of the family for a long time. He may have a problem accepting someone else stepping into that role with you.”

Abby told her she understood and agreed with Cassie. Then she asked Cassie if she thought Jefferson could be interested in someone her age. Cassie laughed at the question. “Oh mother. Have you not seen the way he looks at you? He is already interested. And you are only a few years older than Jefferson. I really do not see that as a problem and if you do, you really need to change your thinking.”

They spoke for quite a while longer. Abby told her daughter about their lunch dates and about the dinners they had shared. She told her about the upcoming estate sale. “I am so looking forward to spending the day with him. I know I am sounding like a teenager with her first crush, but that is how he makes me feel.”

Cassie laughed and tried to reassure her mother about her feelings. “You must be willing to take a chance. You must open your heart and let someone in or else your life will not have any meaning.” Abby listened and told her daughter she sounded like her grandmother. “When I thought about marrying Joseph, I was quite young. My mother gave me the same advice. I did open my heart to your father, and we were happy for a while. I wish I knew why that changed, but since he is gone, I will never find out.”

They ended the call with Cassie advising her to take a chance on love. "If not with Jefferson than someone else. Just do not be afraid to try. You deserve happiness Mom. I love you."

After Cassie hung up Abby sat for a long time and thought about what her daughter had said. "When did she become so smart?" she thought to herself.

Abby went to bed thinking about her daughter and all her good advice. She knew it would take more time for her son to feel the same way about her dating. She decided to not say anything to him until things with Jefferson got more serious. At least she hoped they would.

CHAPTER TWENTY:

Jefferson spent the remainder of his day making plans for his Saturday with Abby. He looked up the time for the sale and made a mental note to let her know when he got to the shop the next day.

He also checked for some places in the country that they could have a nice meal and enjoy the outdoors. The weather was becoming cooler, but there were no storms in the forecast. He made sure he had a warm blanket in the car in case they found a spot to sit and enjoy the scenery. He also put a bottle of wine and some glasses in a basket. He planned to stop on the way home after work to pick up some cheese and crackers.

The next day, he dressed casually for the shop. He only planned to stop by for a few hours to check on Abby and George. When he arrived, he saw quite a few customers browsing the items in the shop. Abby looked up and saw him walk in the front door. She was helping a woman who was interested in one of the large breakfronts.

He nodded to her as he passed and walked to the office. He saw George was completing a sale with a couple who were leaving with some lamps. "Good morning, George. Looks like business is really picking up lately. Must be the new addition to our shop. She does seem to brighten up the place."

George nodded and smiled at Jefferson's comment. "Yes sir, she certainly does. If I can say so, I am glad you realize how much she has brought to the shop. Her enthusiasm seems to rub off on even the customers. She will walk up to someone and before you know it, she knows exactly what they are looking for. It is like your father's technique. Something very impressive to watch."

Jefferson agreed with him. He had noticed that ability also in Abby. That was one of the reasons he thought the shop would thrive with her in charge. As they stood talking, Abby walked over wearing a huge smile. "Good morning, Jefferson. Did you see that lady I was talking to? She just purchased that huge piece that we have been moving around for weeks. She had me set up a delivery date and she paid in full. Isn't that something?"

Jefferson laughed at her excitement. "I do believe Miss Abby that you could sell ice to an Eskimo." They all laughed at George's reaction. He walked out of the office and left them still laughing. Abby turned to Jefferson. "What exactly does that mean?" she asked.

"George was giving you the highest of compliments. He is impressed as am I with your ability to lead the customers to exactly what they want. Even if they are not aware when they walk in through the door. They are all extremely satisfied when they walk out. A quality that my father had, and I saw it in you from the first day on the floor."

Abby blushed and thanked him for his comment. "From what I have heard about your father that is one of the nicest things I could hear."

They chatted for a while and Jefferson told her the time of the sale. He said he would pick her up at ten in the morning on Saturday. He told her to dress warm and bring or wear comfortable shoes. The sale was informal and only open to dealers. She told him she was looking forward to finding some great items for the shop.

He told her since everything seemed in control with the shop he was going to leave. She told him to have a good day and walked out to take care of a new customer.

Jefferson watched her as she approached a well-dressed couple who were just browsing. "They are going to leave after buying something they did not realize they needed or wanted." he thought to himself as he walked outside. Smiling he got in his car and drove back home. He had a few chores to attend to at the house. The next day was Saturday, and he could not wait to pick her up and spend the entire day trying to get closer to her.

Abby looked at Jefferson as he backed his car out of the parking space. She wished the day would go by faster so she could prepare for Saturday. When she thought about being alone with Jefferson her body seemed to take over. She could feel her cheeks beginning to flush and her heart started beating faster.

George walked over with a couple who were interested in a new set of chairs for their den. "This is our new owner Mrs. Sampson. She has quite the eye for design. I am sure if you explain what you are looking for, she can point you to the perfect chairs." They thanked him as Abby led them over to some chairs on display.

George had noticed the expression on her face when she watched Jefferson leave the shop. He knew the next day might prove to be interesting to both. Smiling to himself, he proceeded to the back of the shop and started rearranging some items.

CHAPTER TWENTY-ONE:

Abby drove home from the shop feeling tired but pleased with all the sales they had completed. She thought about George's comment to her about being a good salesperson. She did seem to have a knack for pointing the customer in the right direction even if they did not know themselves. She had always enjoyed decorating, even as a little girl. She would spend hours playing with the dollhouse her father had made. She loved to arrange the rooms differently each day. He would laugh when he saw her sitting on the floor of her room totally lost in her own world of dolls.

She had kept the large dollhouse for years even after she was too old to play. It sat in the attic for a few years while she was in high school. She decided to keep it when she married Joseph. The day they moved into the big house, she visited her parents and retrieved it from the attic. She hoped some day she would have a daughter who would appreciate the house.

When Cassie got old enough, she brought the dollhouse down from the attic and placed it in the corner of her bedroom. Cassie was only a toddler but was overjoyed with the dolls and the furniture. Abby would sit on the floor with her, and they would have hours of fun putting the dolls and the furniture inside.

When Cassie got too old to play with the dollhouse, it again was placed in the attic. Her father had done an excellent job when he built the house. She hoped someday it would find a new home with one of her grandchildren.

The evening passed by slower than Abby would have liked. She had pulled the clothes out of her closet for the next day. She had a new pair of boots that would go perfect with her wool slacks and sweater.

She found a scarf that would add some color to the outfit. Along with a wool blazer she decided she would be comfortable and warm.

Lying in bed that night she found it hard to fall asleep. She kept thinking about what treasures they might find at the sale. Even as she tried to concentrate on the shop, her thoughts kept going back to Jefferson. She could not help but be excited about the prospect of spending the day with him.

When morning finally came, she was up before seven. As she sat having her morning coffee, she watched a bird outside the window. The bright red cardinal appeared to be watching her from his perch on a nearby tree limb.

She thought about the old saying that a cardinal was the spirit of a loved one coming to say hello. She felt it was a good sign whether the saying was true or not.

She finished breakfast and wasted no time with her shower. She was dressed and ready to go when she saw the time was only eight-thirty. She decided to try and concentrate on the novel she was reading, but found she was just reading the same page repeatedly. It seemed like the hands of the clock were not moving at all.

When she finally looked up and saw it was ten, she went to get her jacket and purse. As she passed the front door, she saw Jefferson's car in her driveway. She waited for a few minutes and then walked outside. He saw her and hurried out of the car to meet her.

"How long have you been waiting?" she asked. He laughed and looked down at his feet. "Guess I was anxious to get our day started. I drove around the block a few times before I pulled into the drive." She shook her head and laughed as he held the car door open for her.

"I thought I was the anxious one. All I could think about was getting to the sale before all the good items were already gone." He smiled as he backed out of the driveway.

They both had the same thoughts as they drove down the street. They had not been thinking about the sale at all. Rather, they were anxious to spend the day together.

When Jefferson arrived at the large Victorian house, Abby could not help but be impressed. "What a wonderful house." He agreed with her comment. "Yes. The same family lived here for most of their lives. I can remember driving by with my father a few times. He would always remark about the beautiful antiques they had inside. He had been inside once with my mother to a Christmas party when I was young."

Abby listened to his story. "I hope they still have those beautiful antiques. I look forward to getting our hands on some of them."

They walked up the steps and followed some others inside the large foyer. Abby tried to compose herself when she saw how grand the house was inside. She thought she would love to just run off and look in every room, but she knew that would not be proper. She followed Jefferson and tried to keep her excitement down to a minimum.

The auctioneer welcomed the crowd of buyers. He instructed them as to the rooms that had items for sale. Abby was pleased to hear both the downstairs and the upstairs had items to see. She followed Jefferson into the library. She was quite impressed with the number of books that were displayed. She noticed some first editions that were for sale. Jefferson looked closer at them and told her the prices seemed quite reasonable.

They inspected the large desk and chair. It was a beautiful carved piece that had a high price tag attached. Abby made a mental note to keep watch to see if the auction pushed the price down on any items.They worked their way through the rooms. She noticed a few pieces in the dining room that would bring a decent price in the shop.

The dinnerware that was displayed was a perfect setting for eight. She had some inquiries lately from customers looking for large settings of good china. She told Jefferson and he made a note for the actual sale. After inspecting all the rooms on the lower level, they walked up the beautiful staircase to the bedrooms.

Abby walked into the first room and fell in love with the furnishings. They did not carry a large amount of bedroom items in the shop, and she had been thinking of adding some pieces to their inventory. She looked each piece over very carefully and noted the prices.

Jefferson stood watching her inspect the furniture. "Are you thinking the same thing that I am?" he inquired. She smiled and answered, "I believe so." She told him about her thoughts of expanding their inventory to include bedroom furniture. She told him that quite a few of the customers lately were looking to re-decorate their master bedrooms. The pieces she saw in the house would be perfect for what her customers had in mind.

Jefferson noted the pieces and their prices. He told Abby they would investigate acquiring some of the dressers for the shop. He agreed with her about carrying some different pieces. They had sold quite a lot of their dining room inventory and he thought she made a good point by wanting to include more bedroom furniture.

After inspecting all the bedrooms, they went back downstairs to find the auctioneer talking to a small group of buyers. As they stopped to listen, they heard some people talking about the large barn in the rear of the property. He told them there were some older pieces stored in the building.

When Jefferson heard his comment, he asked if they could look through the barn. The auctioneer told him that would be possible. As they walked out through the kitchen door, they noticed a few others following behind them.

The barn was located at the edge of the back garden. It looked like it had not been kept up very well and when Jefferson opened the large door, they were surprised to see the inside was in incredibly good condition.

"Well looks like they kept the inside cleaned out much better than I expected," he told Abby. The others in the group agreed with him. They all spread out in search of some treasures that might have been overlooked in the inventory for the sale.

Abby looked over the many pieces of furniture. She noticed a small secretary desk pushed behind some other larger pieces. As she walked over to look at it closer, Jefferson followed. "Did you find a piece that looked interesting?" he asked her.

She nodded. "I am not sure. I want to get a closer look. Jefferson moved the desk out from behind the larger piece so she could see it better." While she was inspecting the desk, he stood back and observed the way she touched the piece. It seemed like it might have some value to her at least.

The wood needed some attention. Abby felt it could be brought back to its original beauty with the right person. There was no price tag attached that they could find. Jefferson asked her if she really thought it was valuable enough for the shop.

Abby looked at him. "I was thinking about buying it for myself. It would look lovely in my den by the big window near my fireplace. I have always wanted a piece like this. I think I could really repair it to its original splendor." He saw the look on her face and told her he was going back inside for a few minutes.

She continued to look around the barn but did not find anything that looked promising for the shop. As she turned to walk back to the house, she saw Jefferson walking towards her with the auctioneer. He smiled at her as he led the man over to the desk.

She stood back and watched as they spoke for a few minutes. When the auctioneer walked past her towards the house he smiled and nodded. Jefferson came up behind her and took her by the hand. She looked down to see he had given her the receipt for the desk.

"What is this? Did you buy the desk?" He laughed. "Well, you seemed quite taken by that piece of furniture. I talked the auctioneer into an exceptionally fair price. Consider it a gift for all the great business you have brought into the shop. My father would approve."

They watched as a large man walked into the barn and lifted the desk. "Show me which car is yours sir and I will carry it over for you," he said to Jefferson. As she followed the men to Jefferson's vehicle, she remained speechless. "What a wonderful gift," she thought to herself. More reassurance of what a wonderful person Jefferson was.

As he watched the desk being lifted into his vehicle, Jefferson noticed the smile on Abby's face. He was overjoyed to see how pleased she was with his gesture. He thought the day was only going to improve.

CHAPTER TWENTY-TWO:

When Jefferson had driven away from the house, Abby finally turned to him. "I am so thankful for this wonderful day. You took me off guard by that purchase. I really do not know how to thank you." Jefferson looked at her and smiled. Even though he knew how she could thank him, he only said, "You are very welcome."

They drove in silence for a short way before Jefferson remarked about how many beautiful items they had seen. She agreed and told him she was looking forward to the actual auction. "Do you think we have money to purchase some of the things we picked?" He told her the shop had been doing so well lately that re-stocking their inventory would not be a problem.

"Besides, I want to see how you can talk your customers into the new bedroom furnishings." She looked at him and laughed. "I do not talk anyone into buying anything. I just steer them towards something I think they will like. The items usually sell themselves."

The drive through the countryside proved to be very relaxing. Jefferson saw a small clearing off the road and pulled the car onto it. There was a stream flowing just beyond the spot and he told her it looked like a good place to rest and enjoy the scenery. While he got the blanket and basket of food out of the car, Abby walked over closer to the stream.

When she turned around, he had spread the blanket on the bank. She saw the basket holding the wine bottle and glasses. He reached out his hand to her and helped her down onto the blanket. Watching as he opened the wine and poured their glasses, Abby could not keep from noticing how romantic the setting was.

"Looks like you thought of everything," she told him. He handed her a glass of wine and reached over with his glass. "Here is to a beautiful day spent with a beautiful companion," he said as he touched her glass with his.

They sat taking in the beautiful setting before them. In the distance they saw a field of cows grazing quietly. The birds were singing above them. Abby thought she had not had this wonderful a day in a long time.

"Jefferson. Thank you again for the gift of that desk. It is more than I could have expected." He smiled at her. "Abby, I plan on giving you many more happy moments if you will let me." She was surprised at his comment and not knowing how to answer, she just drank her wine. He noticed her hand shaking and took hold of it with his. "I know this might come as a surprise to you. We have not known each other for a long time. I have begun to realize my feelings for you are much deeper than just our business relationship. Abby. I have been looking forward to spending time alone with you so much. I understand if you are not feeling the same towards me. We could just enjoy each other's company and not speak about this again. If that is what you choose."

Abby sat looking at his handsome face and finally spoke. "Jefferson. I have been looking forward to this day also. My feelings for you have grown much more than I ever expected. I know there is an age difference between us."

Before she could continue, he leaned over and kissed her softly. He pulled back to see her eyes were still closed. "I am sorry if that was too forward. I have wanted to kiss you for quite some time." When she finally opened her eyes, she began to smile at him.

He reached over and took her hand. They sat looking at each other without speaking. When Jefferson leaned over and put his arms around her, she felt her heart beating faster. She could not believe he had feelings for her. His arms felt so strong holding her that she thought she wanted to stay in this moment forever.

They sat on the blanket wrapped in each other's embrace for what seemed like hours. Jefferson looked down into her face and kissed her again. This time with much more passion. She felt his tongue work its way into her mouth and found hers doing the same. His kiss stirred a feeling in her that she had not known for years. It seemed even more intense than the feelings she had for Joseph.

The time seemed to stop moving forward for them. Neither of them realized it had started getting darker. When Abby finally looked up from his kisses, she saw the most beautiful sunset. "Oh Jefferson. Look at that sky. Have you ever seen anything so beautiful?" He laughed as he looked down at her. "Why yes, I have." he remarked.

CHAPTER TWENTY-THREE:

"You must be getting hungry," Jefferson said to Abby. "Since the sun is setting the time must be getting along. Should we find some place to have a quiet dinner?" Abby was still breathless from the passionate kisses. She nodded her head in agreement.

Jefferson stood and helped Abby from the blanket. They gathered their items and headed to his car. Abby's mind was spinning. Had they just both enjoyed some wildly intense kissing? She was afraid she would wake to find it was only a dream.

Driving further along the dark highway, Jefferson glanced over and noticed how quiet Abby was being. "Is everything all right Abby?" he asked her. "Yes," she said. Feeling very confused and fragile, she did not make any more conversation.

When they reached a quaint looking restaurant, Jefferson pulled into the lot. "This looks promising. Want to try it?" She told him it looked fine to her and followed him inside. When they had been seated Jefferson looked over at her and was beginning to think he had been too aggressive earlier. Maybe she did not really feel the same and he had pushed her too fast. Should he say anything or just wait until she was ready?

As his thoughts were racing, Abby excused herself and went to the restroom. Once inside, she leaned on the counter. She looked at her reflection in the mirror. "What am I doing? Jefferson does seem to have feelings for me. Those kisses proved there was some attraction. Should I go any further?" She tried to compose herself before going back to their table.

Jefferson sat alone wondering about his earlier actions and words. He was certain he had moved too fast with Abby. He knew she had been alone for some time since her husband had died. Maybe she still was not ready for a relationship. Maybe she had just been friendly at the shop because she wanted to become the new owner.

He saw her walking back across the room. She looked at him and smiled. He was almost ready to say they should leave when she stopped and leaned down to kiss his cheek. When she sat back in her chair, he could see she looked more relaxed. "I am sorry about earlier. Your words took me by surprise. I was not prepared for you to show me such affection. Please forgive me. You must think I am acting like a silly teenager experiencing her first crush."

Jefferson smiled back at her and took her hand. "Abby. The only thing I was thinking is that I went too fast. I was afraid I scared you away. That is the last thing that I want. I want to get closer to you. I know you had an unpleasant experience with your husband. I do not want you to be worried about my affections towards you. You are the most thoughtful and wonderful woman that I have met in an exceptionally long time. You show such passion about the shop. I did not plan to let my feelings run away, but when you were so close, I could not stop myself. Please tell me I did not ruin everything before it even got started."

Abby listened to Jefferson and saw the concern on his face. "I feel the same way, Jefferson. I have been trying not to have any feelings for you for a while now. I was so worried that you would reject any involvement with me because of our age difference." He started to laugh. "Wow. I am so relieved. I do have stronger feelings for you Abby than even I realized. Those kisses we shared made me well aware of just how deep those feelings are. As far as our ages. Just how old do you think I am?"

Abby began to blush at his words. "I guess I thought you were only in your forties." He laughed and held her hand tighter. "My sweet Abby. I am fifty-three years old. See? You are younger than I am." She was shocked at the revelation. "What? Well then will you please let me know where that fountain of youth is located."

They sat at the table holding hands and laughing when the waiter arrived with their drinks. "I ordered a glass of wine when you went to the restroom. I hope that is all right," he told her. "That is fine. Thank you." As the waiter left the table, she added "I think I really need this wine to clear my head and stop it from spinning."

Their dinners arrived and they enjoyed the rest of the evening with conversation about the estate sale. Jefferson informed her the actual sale was scheduled for Monday at ten in the morning. He told her he could meet her at the shop, and they could drive to the sale together. She asked if George would be able to handle the shop by himself.

Jefferson said he had decided to give George a long weekend including Monday. He had called George the night before and told him the plans. Abby was pleased and surprised that he was willing to close the shop for an extra day.

They finished their meal and after coffee and dessert, they walked out to Jefferson's car. Before she could get inside, he put his arms around her. "Everything all right with us now?" he asked. Abby smiled. "Yes, more than all right. Everything is perfect." she responded as she touched his lips with hers.

CHAPTER TWENTY-FOUR:

The drive home seemed to go by too fast for them. The conversation was much lighter than earlier. Jefferson told her about more of his travels abroad. She listened intently to his every word. She was still finding it hard to believe that she was two years younger than he was.

Abby and Joseph had married young. She had her children when she was only in her early thirties. Now she was a young grandmother of fifty-one. She had to admit that Jefferson's kisses made her feel much younger.

When they got to her house Jefferson opened her car door. They walked up the steps together and he waited while she unlocked the front door. When she turned to him, he took her in his arms. His kiss was gentler than she had ever experienced with Joseph. There was no urgency in his arms just a feeling of safety. When he released her from his embrace, he looked into her eyes. "Abby, I have enjoyed every minute of our day together. Even the uncertain ones." She told him she felt the same way.

He turned to walk back to his car, and she thought he was leaving without saying good night. Then she realized she had forgotten about the desk in the back of his car. When he carried it up on the porch, she held the door open for him. "Where would you like this?" he asked.

She told him he could leave it in the hallway. "I will decide tomorrow where the best place would be to refinish and clean the piece." He nodded and placed it in a corner out of the way from the door. "Well, this evening must end. I will call you tomorrow to see if you need any help moving the desk."

She thanked him again for the wonderful gift. He kissed her again and then walked down the steps to his car. She watched him drive away before she closed the door.

She locked the door and went upstairs to her bedroom. After changing into her pajamas, she crawled under the covers. She reached for her phone and saw a few missed calls from her daughter.

She noticed the last one was only a half hour before, so she decided to call Cassie. The phone was answered on the first ring. "Mom. I have been calling you. I am afraid I have something to tell you that is going to be upsetting."

Abby listened while her daughter told her about speaking to Henry. Cassie had informed him about Abby's relationship with Jefferson. "He did not take the news very well, I'm afraid." Abby was not too surprised when she heard of her son's obvious misgivings. She had expected him to react in just such a way. "It is all right Cassie. Please do not let this bother you. I already knew what Henry was going to say about the idea of me dating Jefferson or anyone else for that matter. I will call him in the morning, and we can talk over his objections."

"Oh mom, I am sorry. I should not have said anything to him. Please forgive me." Abby told her that there was no problem and no apologies necessary. Cassie asked her how the day went with Jefferson. She proceeded to tell her about the sale and the desk he had purchased for her. She hesitated about filling her in on their kisses later while near the stream. "Some things should be kept private," she thought.

Before they ended the call, she told Cassie about finding out his age. Laughing Cassie responded to her discovery. "Well see Mom. Now there is nothing standing in your way. Are you going to go forward with your attraction to him?"

Abby told her she needed to think about it overnight. She promised to call her the next day and tell her about the call to Henry. She hung up the call and lay in bed for a long time before sleep finally arrived.

When Cassie ended the call with her mother, she joined her husband in bed. "Who was on the phone this late?" Jake asked her. "It was Mom. She just got home from her day with Jefferson." He asked her how everything went at the sale. "Well, they had an exceptionally good day together. And even though she did not say anything specifically, I have a feeling she found the attraction to be mutual on Jefferson's part as well. I could hear something in her voice." He leaned on his elbow and looked at his wife. "What do you mean? What did you hear?" Cassie smiled. "Happiness. That is what I heard. She sounded happier than she has in an awfully long time. The news about Henry did not even seem to take away her happiness."

Jake leaned over and kissed Cassie good night. She lay in bed thinking about Abby and the day she spent with Jefferson. She hoped she was correct with her thinking. She could not be more pleased for her mother. This man could be the answer to ending her mother's loneliness. She certainly hoped so. Plus, she would ring her brother's neck if he tried to ruin everything for their mother.

CHAPTER TWENTY-FIVE:

Abby woke the next morning feeling more rested than she had for a long time. She thought about her day with Jefferson. She could still feel the warmth of his kisses.

She dressed in sweats and went downstairs. While she waited for the coffee to be brewed, she went to look at the desk. She thought she should move it out to the enclosed porch off the kitchen. She did not want to try to carry it down to the cellar for fear of dropping the piece. It already had some noticeable dings and dents. No sense in adding more that had to be repaired.

When she tried to pick it up, she was surprised at how heavy the piece was. "I did not expect that," she thought. Thinking for a moment she decided to grab a towel and once she had lifted the front legs onto the towel, she was able to pull it under the back. This allowed her to pull the desk along the hallway without scratching the wood floor.

She had to lift it a little at the step down to the porch. By only lifting one side at a time, she managed without any accidents. She moved the desk over near the windows so she could use the light to really inspect the damage.

Abby decided to pull out the small drawer in the middle of the desk. Once it was removed, she turned it over and found a small brown envelope taped underneath. When she opened the envelope, she could not believe what she found inside.

She checked the time and saw it was not too early to call Jefferson. He answered almost immediately. "Good morning, Abby. I was just sitting here having my coffee and thinking about you." She waited for him to finish. "Good morning, Jefferson. I was wondering if you were busy today. I found something that I think you will find as extraordinary as I do."

"Well in fact. I was going to stop by later to see if you would like to go to brunch with me." She told him that sounded wonderful, and the call ended.

Abby went upstairs to shower and change her clothes. She could not wait for Jefferson to arrive. Not only because she wanted to spend more time with him, but she was interested to see his reaction over her discovery.

When she finished her shower, she decided to call Henry before his day got too far along. "Hello mom. How are you?" he asked when he answered. "Hello Henry. I am fine thanks. Hope you and the family are doing well. We have something we need to discuss."

Henry did not respond to her comment. Abby continued. "Henry, I know you have felt like the man of our family since your father died. I also know you have enough obligations with your own family to manage without worrying about me. I have found that I have feelings for Jefferson and that he feels the same for me. I do not know where this friendship will lead. I would feel better knowing my children are behind my decision to finally start dating. Your father has been gone for quite some time now. And as I am sure you and Cassie are aware of how our marriage had gone downhill long before his death. I am still a young woman and I need companionship. Someone to spend my time with and fall in love again."

He was silent for a few minutes after trying to digest his mother's words. "But mom. How much do you really know about this man? I worry that he will take advantage of you. I just want you to be happy and to find someone who could be in your life. Do you really think that person is Jefferson Matthews?"

"Yes Henry. I believe he might be. We have been seeing each other casually outside of the shop. He has opened my eyes to a great big world that is full of possibilities. Working at the shop has been so wonderful for my self-esteem. We are doing quite well with new customers every day. I am enjoying having something to wake up to every day. Please try to understand Henry. I have never been someone to jump into any situation without thinking it through. I thought you had more faith in my judgement."

He agreed with her words. He said she had always been a person who was levelheaded with any problems they might have. He finally agreed to withhold his opinion about Jefferson. "I will not say anything more about this new man in your life. But mom. If he does hurt you in anyway, he will have to deal with me."

She laughed and told him that he had nothing to be concerned about. "I plan to take this friendship slow. I am not going to jump into bed with the first man who shows me some attention."

Henry was shocked. "Mother! I really do not want to have that discussion with my own mother." She teased him and they both had a laugh before the call ended.

She walked over to refill her coffee when the doorbell rang. She saw Jefferson standing on the porch as she walked down the hall. "Well, did you fly here?" He smiled and grabbed her in his arms. "I am afraid I could not wait another minute before doing this." He pulled her closer and his kiss was as passionate as the day before.

She found it difficult to catch her breath afterwards. He put his arm around her waist as they walked into the kitchen. "I was just having my second cup of coffee. Would you like some?"

He nodded and sat down at the island watching her pour his coffee. "I have to admit that aside from missing you I am very interested in this amazing thing you have to tell me."

She sat down on the stool next to him and started to drink her coffee. Finally, he looked over at her. "How long are you going to torment me before you tell me your secret?"

Abby laughed at the look on his face. "I may wait a little longer since I am really enjoying watching your face. I promise you it will be worth the wait."

CHAPTER TWENTY-SIX:

Henry sat thinking about the phone conversation with his mother. He knew everything she had said was true. He had taken on the role of man of the house after his father's death. He felt very protective of his sister and his mother.

She had always been the parent that was present with her children. He loved his father, but his family always took second place to everything else in his life. He realized as he got older how important it was to work hard and provide for your family. There was one difference between him and his father. His wife, Alice and their children were always his top priority.

He enjoyed coming home from an exhausting day at the office to find his wife waiting with open arms. She would always take time to listen to him while he discussed any problems that had arisen at work. She would make him feel special regardless of how tired she was from chasing their three-year-old son. He remembered how thrilled he was when she informed him about being pregnant with their second child.

When she gave birth to a beautiful baby girl, he felt like their family was complete. He looked down at that little face after Alice handed him their new daughter. She was the most beautiful thing he had ever seen. He only hoped she grew up looking as lovely as her mother.

Henry remembered when his younger sister Cassie was born. They were only four years apart, but he immediately took on the role of big brother. He loved watching her grow into a strong, confident woman. Cassie had known Jake since childhood. Henry was so proud to see her walk down the aisle.

Now that she was going to give him a niece or nephew, he could not be happier for her and Jake. He knew how much they had wanted to start a family. It seemed to come very naturally to him and Alice. Cassie had told him that she worried that she would not be able to give her husband a family. He understood their excitement and joy when she discovered she was finally pregnant with their first child.

Abby had been so understanding of him when he was growing up. His father always was too busy or pre-occupied with other things to notice his good grades. He remembered seeing his mother at all his baseball games. He could not remember his father even seeing him play once.

He sat watching Hank play with his trucks and knew when he was old enough to be into sports that he would be in the stands. There would be no meeting more important than supporting his child in whatever activities they participated in during school.

Henry looked up as Alice walked into the family room carrying Annie. She stood by the door and smiled at her husband. "Whatcha doing?" she asked. He smiled back and reached out for Annie. "Just enjoying my son. Come sit by me." Alice handed over Annie and sat down on the floor next to Henry's chair.

"I heard you on the phone with your mother earlier," she said to him. He nodded. "Yes, she called to talk to me about Jefferson." Alice listened as he told her about the call. "Sounds like she is beginning to start a new phase in her life. I am happy for her. You do not look like you feel the same way."

Henry looked at her and shook his head. "I listened to what she told me. I heard the words and agreed with them. But I still cannot stop worrying about her. I know she is a levelheaded woman. I also know she does not do anything without thinking it through from all sides."

"Well, then how did you leave the call with her. Are you willing to stay in the background and allow her to lead her life the way she wants?" He smiled, "I agreed to try. However, you can be certain I am going to keep a close eye on Jefferson. He did seem like a nice man, but no one will ever be good enough for my mother."

Alice reached up and took his hand. "Yes, I am sure of that my love. That is partly why I fell in love with you. Any guy who thinks as much for his mother has to be someone that can be trusted with your heart." Henry leaned down and kissed her on the forehead. They both looked up when Hank started to laugh. "Daddy's kissing mommy." he said as he pointed at his parents.

Alice went over and grabbed Hank. Hugging and kissing the little boy until he started to squirm, they all laughed. Even Annie joined in and gurgled and cooed in her father's arms. Henry thought to himself how blessed he was to have such a wonderful life.

CHAPTER TWENTY-SEVEN:

Abby watched Jefferson frown as he waited for her to tell him what secret she had discovered. "You are enjoying this, right?" he said to her. She nodded and waited a few more minutes before going to the kitchen counter. She turned to him and held out her hand. When she turned it over, he saw the key she held in her palm.

For a moment he did not understand. Then when he looked closer to the key, he saw the definite shape. "Is that the key to the trunk at the shop? It certainly looks like the right shape." Abby nodded. "Yes, I believe it is just that."

Jefferson took the key and examined it closely. "Where did you get this?" She told him about the envelope that had been taped to the bottom of the desk drawer. He looked up with the same surprised expression that she had when she found it. "How can that be?"

Abby told him she had no clue what the connection was between the desk and the trunk. She asked him if his father had any documents regarding the trunk or who had left it at the shop years before.

Jefferson told her he had looked through some of the files at the shop but did not find anything. Since he was still living in his father's house, they both decided to look there for any clues. "He may have some papers in his desk that will shine some light on this mystery. We should try to find out if the desk belonged to the owner of the estate. It might have been in that barn when they moved into the house and never noticed it before."

They decided to have brunch at the local café before driving to Jefferson's home. While they ate Abby talked about the possibility of such a discovery. "I have to admit that I love a good mystery." she said as she smiled at Jefferson.

Without saying the words, he thought to himself that he was starting to have strong feelings for her. He did not want to rush things and scare her, so he kept the realization to himself. "At least for now," he thought.

The drive to Jefferson's house was only a short distance from the café. Abby felt excited over the prospect of finding some clues about the owner of the trunk. At least she hoped they could find out when the trunk was brought to the shop.

She was surprised at the size of the house when they pulled into the driveway. "Oh, what a beautiful home," she told Jefferson. "Thanks. It has been my family home for a few generations. I think my great-grandfather had it built sometime in the early nineteenth century."

He parked in the large driveway and held the car door open for her. She followed him up the steps and found a beautiful, decorated entryway accented with a large staircase.

As they walked inside, she looked around at all the paintings on the walls leading up the stairs. Jefferson led her into his father's study which was on the right off the main hall.

She looked at the walls covered with bookcases. "Your father must have loved books," she said. Jefferson nodded. "He had brought some of them into the shop for sale. The ones in the attic that were in the trunk that your son found, were some of his collections. He would bring home any new ones that came into his possession first before he decided to sell them. He knew the value of many of them and had a few collectors he would contact if he found something they might be interested in before he placed them in the shop.

Jefferson sat down at the large desk and Abby took a chair in front. "I thought this would be a good place to start our search. He usually filed most of his important documents, but sometimes he just put them in the desk and forgot about them.

As they looked through the many papers they found, Abby found Jefferson sneaking a look her way every now and then. He started to smile when she caught his glances. "Sorry. I just cannot stop looking at your beautiful face Abby." He put down the paper he held and reached for her hand. "Have you thought about our trip the other day?"

Abby told him it had been on her mind constantly. He smiled. "Good. I was worried about your feelings after I left your house. I really want to get to know you better. Please let me know if you think I am being too forward. The last thing I want to do is chase you away."

"Jefferson. I told you I have feelings for you also. I think getting better acquainted with each other should be our priority. We are already friends. I have not dated very often since Joseph's death. I appreciate you allowing me the time I need to understand my feelings. I assure you that you have not chased me away. I enjoyed our day together. I think the kisses we shared show just how much we are beginning to feel for each other. I would really like to explore this relationship further."

CHAPTER TWENTY-EIGHT:

Abby sat thinking about Jefferson's words. She knew her feelings were getting stronger. She wanted to ignore her hesitation and run into his arms. Something still held her back. Was it fear of being hurt again? Why did she not trust herself?

"Abby, I know you are hesitant because of your past with Joseph. All I can say is that I am not Joseph. I want to get closer to you, but I will not ever push you into doing anything you do not feel comfortable doing. My feelings are too strong to ever hurt you, Abby. Please believe that."

He did not say anything more but went back to looking through the desk. Abby walked around the large room inspecting the many books. She came across one that took her attention. It was a book with the picture of a beautiful schooner on the cover. She pulled the book off the shelf and when she opened it a paper fell to the floor. She bent to pick it up and when she opened the paper she stopped and looked up at Jefferson.

"Jefferson. You must see this." He walked over to her and took the paper from her hand. When he started to read it, he was shocked. It was a note to his father. The note referred to the trunk and it was signed by someone called Captain Warren.

"This is incredible. I do not ever remember my father knowing or even speaking about anyone by that name. The note sounds like they were old acquaintances. He is the one who owned that trunk originally. It still does not explain how the trunk came to be in my father's shop. We must dig further to find out who this man was and what the connection was to my father."

They spent a few hours scouring over the papers in the desk. Abby looked through some more of the books to see if she could find any more clues. Finally, Jefferson sat back in his chair. "I don't think we are going to find anything else here," he said to Abby.

She walked over to him, "did your father keep any papers about the shop anywhere else in the house? In another room or the attic?" Jefferson looked up at her and suddenly remembered seeing some old trunks in the attic. "Possibly. When I was younger, I would go up to the attic. I remember seeing some old trunks there. We should have a look. Do you want to dig further into this mystery? I do not want to take up your time if you have other things you need to take care of today."

She shook her head. "Do you think I would miss a chance to solve this mystery. I am having the time of my life looking for more clues to the trunk, the key in my desk and this Captain Warren." He smiled at her and taking her hand he led her upstairs to the attic. She was surprised when he opened the door. She expected to see a musty room filled with cobwebs. Instead, she saw inside a very cozy well-kept space. There were a few comfortable chairs against the wall with a table and lamp between them. There was an old worn but clean antique rug on the floor. Along the opposite wall were a few filing cabinets. She looked further and saw the trunks that Jefferson had mentioned.

"This is nothing like I expected to find. What a lovely spot. I can see why you would enjoy coming here when you were a boy." He nodded. "I would come up here and read. It always felt like a safe place. I could block out the outside world and get lost in a book."

Abby was trying to envision Jefferson sitting in one of the chairs reading. She knew it would have appealed to her to do the same. She would have loved having a quiet space to relax when she was a child.

Her life had not always been peaceful when she was younger. Her parents were loving to her and each other. However, they did have some very verbal arguments. She always got sent to her room, but it was still close enough to hear the accusations and threats her parents threw at one another. "Abby? Are you ok?" She looked up and realized Jefferson was talking to her. "Oh, I am sorry. Just lost in a memory. Yes, I am fine. I really like this room. It feels quite safe and comfortable." He agreed and walked over to the trunks.

"Let us check these out first. While I look. you inspect the filing cabinets. I do not know if my father filed anything up here or not." She nodded and walked over to the closest cabinet. Inside she only found a few store receipts from when the shop was run by Jefferson's grandfather. She looked through them but did not see anything referencing anyone named Captain Warren.

Jefferson knelt on the floor near one of the trunks. He pulled out some old clothes and jewelry boxes. Beneath the piles he found a brown leather folder. As he opened it, he gasped. "Abby. Look at this."

She knelt beside him as he showed her the folder. Inside were maps and letters. They were all signed with the name Captain Warren. "The lighting is not good enough to look through these. We can bring them downstairs and read them better. This is exactly what we are hunting for." Abby followed him as he went back down the stairs. They settled on the sofa in the den and Jefferson pulled out the papers he had found.

CHAPTER TWENTY-NINE:

The afternoon went along with Abby and Jefferson reading the letters they had found from Captain Warren. Some of them were to his grandfather John. There were a few to a woman named Elizabeth. Those were the most interesting and confusing.

The letters to John showed that he had been friends with the captain for some time. Since they were young men. Jefferson told Abby he never remembered hearing any stories referencing Captain Warren or a woman named Elizabeth Hemmings.

The last letter they found in the trunk mentioned the secretary desk. It had originally belonged to Captain Warren, but he had given it to his betrothed Elizabeth Hemmings. Jefferson stopped reading and looked at Abby. "That was the name of the former owner of the mansion where the sale was held. She must have been the woman involved with the captain. We should look up in the old newspaper files to see if there was any mention of her or the captain. She must never have married since her last name was still the same."

They finished the letter but did not find any further information. "Well that explains how the key came to be in the desk," he said to Abby. She agreed, "yes, but it still does not tell us where the trunk came from or what is inside."

Jefferson and Abby looked through the remaining trunks and filing cabinets but found no further mention of anything pertaining to the Captain or Elizabeth.

"I guess the only thing to do is try the key and see if it does in fact open the trunk at the shop." Abby nodded. "I am afraid of what we find inside. I just have a strange feeling about this whole thing." She did not explain further. The feeling was just a strong premonition of something bad coming to them.

Jefferson closed the house and drove Abby home. He told her he would pick her up in the morning at her house. They could drive to the sale together and check out the trunk afterwards.

She told him that sounded like a good plan. He kissed her good night and she watched as he backed out of the driveway.

When she closed the house that night, she took extra care to check all the locks. She could not shake the feeling she had. There were only a few times in her life when she felt this way.

The last time was just before she was informed about her husband's sudden death.

CHAPTER THIRTY:

Abby woke early the next day after a restless night. She saw there was a slight dusting of snow outside her window. It made the yard look brighter in the morning sun.

She showered and dressed for their outing. Sitting in the kitchen enjoying her coffee and Danish, she thought about the letters they had found the day before. She wondered why Jefferson's father had never mentioned the captain to him. She also thought about Elizabeth and the relationship she had with the captain. Had they married? If not, why? It appeared from the letters that she was especially important to Captain Warren.

She hoped they would find some additional answers in the trunk at the shop. She looked forward to attending the estate sale, but she was much more interested in the contents of the mysterious trunk.

As she was cleaning the kitchen and her breakfast dishes, she heard a car pull in the driveway. When she looked out the window, she saw Jefferson walking up to the door. He saw her inside and she waved him in. When he tried the door, it was still locked. Laughing she rushed to open it for him. "Sorry. I forgot to unlock the door when I came downstairs this morning."

He leaned down and kissed her. "Good morning. I thought for a moment you were playing games." She smiled, "no Jefferson. We are both too old to play games with each other." He looked at her not exactly sure of her meaning but did not make a comment.

"I just must run upstairs and grab my purse and jacket. Be down in a minute or two." She ran up the stairs as he stood in the hallway and waited for her.

Jefferson liked the inside of this big house. It was not as large as his father's, but it felt more comfortable. He thought that he would be quite contented living here with Abby if their relationship ever got to that point. Of course, he was not sure how her family would feel about him moving into their father's house.

He heard her footsteps coming down the stairs and walked out to the hallway. "Ready?" She nodded and followed him out the front door. She made sure the door was secure and then went to his car. "Are you always so careful about locking the doors?" he asked her.

She looked over at him as they drove out to the street. "I never used to be. I have just been having some strange feelings lately. No harm in being cautious. Especially since I live by myself."

He nodded and they continued to the estate sale. She glanced over at him and saw he had a concerned look on his face. She thought he was preoccupied with the sale. They drove in silence most of the way. When they arrived, she was surprised at the vast number of cars already parked near the mansion.

"Well today should be interesting. Looks like we might have some others interested in the same pieces we previously picked for the shop." They walked inside and after taking a brochure from the usher at the door they were able to find two seats together towards the front of the room.

When they started bringing out the first few items up for sale, Jefferson leaned forward, and Abby knew he had noticed one of the large pieces for the bedroom that they had selected. He just looked at her and motioned towards the furniture but said nothing.

The auctioneer greeted everyone and began the auction. The very first item was a large dresser with an attached mirror. Abby had thought it would be an extremely popular item with some of her recent customers. Jefferson made no attempt to bid until some others had started. The amount was low to start, but quickly climbed to a sizeable figure. Abby was wondering if he intended to bid on the piece. She was thinking about trying to bid herself when he raised his paddle and bid two hundred higher than the current amount.

The auctioneer waited for someone to offer another amount, but no one offered. Within minutes the bidding was closed, and the piece belonged to Jefferson. He reached over and squeezed Abby's hand. "That is a beautiful piece of furniture. I have a feeling we can sell it for much more than you just paid," she told him. "I agree with you," he responded.

The morning continued in the same fashion. There were comparable items they had considered for bedroom sets. Jefferson was able to pick up a genuinely nice mahogany bed and nightstand. The price was slightly higher but again Abby thought it was worth the investment.

The bidding moved to some smaller pieces along with some of the china she had inspected earlier. When the set came up that she had chosen she started bidding on her own. Jefferson was amused at how excited she was when she ended giving the selling bid.

"Oh, I am so pleased. I have a couple who were looking for that exact pattern. They will be thrilled when I contact them. Especially when I tell them about the additional pieces that come with the dishes."

After buying several more items they sat and listened to the other bidders. They both agreed the pieces they purchased had been reasonably priced. Abby bid on a few more glassware sets and was able to obtain one of the large serving platters that she had seen.

The morning slipped by very rapidly. They enjoyed some refreshments that were supplied by the auction house. After a short intermission, the sale lasted another few hours.

Some of the larger furniture sets sold for some extremely unreasonable prices. Jefferson told Abby he felt they were too expensive for the shop. He said they had quite a few sofas and chairs already that needed to be sold before adding to their inventory. Abby agreed with his assessment. She knew he was spending the shop's budget for furniture. They both decided to stop for the day, and she waited outside while he settled payment and arranged for delivery to the shop.

The day was another beautiful fall day. Even though it had started with a light dusting of snow, the sun had melted everything, and the temperature had improved since morning.

"Are we ready to leave?" she asked as he walked over. "Yes ma'am. The items are paid for, and they plan to deliver them on Wednesday." They walked to the car and Jefferson held the door for her. "Do you want to stop for something to eat now or should we continue on to the shop?" he asked her.

"I am not hungry but more anxious to try that key and look inside the trunk," she replied. He agreed and they drove back into town. "Were you pleased with the items we were able to purchase?" he asked her. "Oh yes. We got most of the pieces we had looked at earlier. I think they will be extremely popular with some of our customers. The couple I spoke of before were also looking for bedroom furniture. We could make them a special deal if they bought all the latest items."

CHAPTER THIRTY-ONE:

When Jefferson arrived at the shop he parked in front. Since it was later in the day there were fewer cars parked on the street. Abby opened the front door and turned off the alarm.

Jefferson locked the door behind them, and they walked back to the office to leave their coats before going upstairs. As they climbed the stairs to the attic Abby could not help being apprehensive as to the contents in the trunk. Jefferson knelt and after Abby handed him the key, she waited for him to try the lock.

She held her breath while he turned the key. It was exactly the right one for the old lock. When it turned and the lock opened, they both gasped. "I know you are as excited as I am," he said to her before he raised the lid to the old trunk.

Abby watched and waited as he raised the lid. When the trunk was open for a second the dust inside escaped all at once. When the air cleared around them, they both leaned in to look at the contents. There were some old clothes folded very neatly. Abby saw one of the items was a beautiful lace wedding dress. Beneath the dress was a pair of satin slippers that were laying atop a lovely lace veil.

Jefferson carefully handed the items to Abby who laid them upon a nearby table. He reached in further and pulled out what looked like a sea captain's dress uniform and hat. She added those to the table also. Finally in the bottom of the trunk was a large wooden box. Jefferson pulled it out and saw there was nothing else inside the trunk.

He stood and carried the box over to the table. The box was very beautifully carved. It did not have a lock, so he was able to open it without any problem.

Inside they found a beautiful antique set of pistols. He looked at Abby. "These are dueling pistols. I cannot be certain until I have an expert inspect them. They are in pristine condition. If they are authentic, they could be worth quite a lot of money."

Abby looked at the items laying on the table. "Are you thinking what I am thinking?" she asked Jefferson. "Do you suppose these were to be the wedding clothes for Captain Warren and Elizabeth? And what are the pistols doing locked in the trunk with the clothes? Our mystery is getting increasingly curious with each new discovery."

Jefferson nodded and looked as puzzled as she was. He had no idea what the contents of the trunk explained. He was determined to find out though. He also wanted to know what his father had to do with the entire situation.

Abby inspected the clothes while Jefferson was looking over the pistols. "Jefferson. Look at this." she said as she handed him a small piece of paper. "Where did you find this?" he asked her. "It was in the pocket of the man's coat."

Jefferson unfolded the piece of flimsy paper. He read the note to her. "My darling Elizabeth. I am sorry that our future depends on this drastic act. I cannot allow you to be taken from me by another man. I have loved you for so long. If today's outcome is not in my favor, please always remember how much I care about you." The note was signed Your Love, Arthur.

Abby watched as Jefferson read the note to her. She had such a strong feeling of longing. The room seemed to take on a chill that she had not noticed when they entered. Jefferson stood and handed the note to her. As she reached to take it in her hand, she noticed something near the window.

"Jefferson. What is that?" He turned quickly in the direction she was looking. There on the far side of the room was a strange filmy outline. As they both watched, it became clearer. They both watched as the figure of a woman appeared before them. She did not speak but reached out her hands as if to plead for help. Before either of them could make any movement, she disappeared again.

Abby grabbed the nearby table to steady her shaking body. Jefferson reached for her arm. "Are you alright?" he asked. She nodded. "Did you see her too?" she asked him. Jefferson said that he had seen the woman or what appeared to be a woman.

"Who was she? What does she want? She looked like she was begging for our help." Jefferson said he agreed. "I did not recognize her. Could she have been Elizabeth Hemmings?" Abby told him she felt that was exactly the woman's identity.

"We must look at those old newspapers in the town archives. Perhaps we can find a photo of her. They may also have some explanation as to what happened to her and the captain." He did not add that he hoped it would explain the role his father played in this drama.

Jefferson took her arm and helped her down the attic stairs. "You need to sit down for a few minutes. Then I think we should walk over to the café for something to eat. Maybe if we put our minds together, we can form some sort of explanation for what we both just witnessed."

Abby took his advice and sat down by the desk. Her mind was swirling. How could they have seen a ghost. But that was exactly what had happened.

CHAPTER THIRTY-TWO:

Abby walked with Jefferson across the street to the café. She was not hungry after the bizarre incident they had both witnessed. They sat at the table quietly. Neither of them knew what to say concerning what they had just seen. The waitress walked over, and they both just ordered coffee.

When she left their table, Abby looked at Jefferson. "I think we both could use something stronger than coffee." He nodded in agreement. "I have never had such a strange experience," he told her. Abby thought for a moment before responding. "Remember when you first opened the trunk, and that dust blew out into the room? Well, after what happened, I do not think that was dust. It was the spirit of Elizabeth Hemmings."

Jefferson looked at her in surprise. "Do you really believe that?" She looked upset but quite serious. Nodding her head, she looked down at the table. When she raised her head, he could see her eyes tearing up. He reached out for her hand. "Please do not get upset. We will find the underlying cause of this mystery. I am here with you, and we will face whatever comes next together."

Abby smiled at him and sat quietly while he held her hand. They drank their coffee in silence. The café did not appear too busy which made Abby more comfortable. She had a feeling that someone was already watching. She looked around and saw nothing, but the feeling stayed with her until they left the café.

"Do you want to go to check out those archives now?" he asked her. "We must. I will not be able to concentrate on anything else until we look for further information. He agreed and took her arm as they crossed the street to his car.

The archives for the town's history were housed in the town hall. It was still early enough for them to get their search done before the building closed for the day.

The clerk inside directed them to an area where all the old newspapers were stored. The original copies were available along with microfilm copies. Jefferson thought it would be easier to check the film first. "Then if we find anything important, we can look at the original news articles." She agreed and watched as he started rolling through the films.

They searched for what felt like hours, but in fact the time was much shorter. Jefferson finally stopped when he found an article about a duel between two of the town's most esteemed citizens. He saw the names and knew this was what they were searching for. As he jotted down the date of the article Abby started paging through the piles of newspapers.

She found the correct paper halfway down the stack. "Here Jefferson. This is the one we need." He took the paper to an adjacent table and they both stood while he turned the pages to the article. They noticed several photos were also attached to the article about the duel that was between Captain Arthur Warren and Mr. John Matthews.

Jefferson started reading aloud and when he saw the referenced name of John Matthews, he realized they meant his grandfather. He looked over at Abby before he continued. "The citizens of Cobble Bay were shocked to hear about the duel between Captain Warren and business owner John Matthews. They learned that the duel was over a local woman Miss Elizabeth Hemmings. The men met at a nearby field just after dawn on this fateful day. The only others in attendance were their seconds. After they were informed of the rules for dueling, they each took out one of their pistols and stood back-to-back in the field. After counting off twenty paces, they both turned, aimed, and fired their pistols. Both men fell to the ground. When the seconds went to their aid it was discovered one had survived. Captain Warren laid bleeding on the field after receiving a mortal gunshot wound. Mr. Matthews was taken by his second to the local doctor. He had only suffered a flesh wound to his leg and was taken to his home after receiving treatment.

The local constable was summoned to the home of Mr. Matthews after reports of the duel reached his attention. We received word from a reliable source that the duel was initiated by Captain Warren. There were no charges brought against Mr. Matthews as it was determined he only shot in self-defense. We will report any further developments when this office receives them."

Jefferson sat onto a nearby chair. Abby saw his face had lost all its color. "Are you all right?" she asked him. He was quiet for a while before he responded. "I always knew my grandfather had a slight limp, but I never remember being told why. It must have been from that wound he received."

They sat in silence for a while. Abby watched as Jefferson re-read the article a few more times. She realized this was some of his family history that had never been shared with him. He finally stood and walked over to the films and began looking through them again. "What are you looking for now?" she asked. "I want to see if there was any mention of my grandfather and Elizabeth."

Abby looked at him. "Was your grandmother's name Elizabeth?" He looked up at her and shook his head. "No, her name was Analissa."

Abby did not know how to respond to his answer. If Elizabeth Hemmings was not his grandmother, then who was she? What happened to her? These questions were swimming in her brain while she watched him scan through film after film.

They had been busy and not noticed the time. The clerk walked into the room and told them they were getting ready to close for the day. Jefferson stood and after making a note about the date of the last film he viewed, he thanked the clerk. Abby followed him outside and he did not speak until they were seated in his car.

"Abby, I hope you do not mind if I take you home now. I have a lot of things to sort out and it is best if I were alone for right now." She said that was fine and sat quietly as they drove to her house. She got out of his car, and they walked to the front door together. "Thank you for a very interesting and unusual day," she said.

He kissed her cheek and told her goodbye. She waved as he backed onto the street and drove away. "She knew he was upset over the news he had uncovered about his family. She decided to give him time to digest all the information about his grandfather. She thought they would discuss the articles further the next day when they arrived at the shop.

Abby was surprised when Jefferson did not come to the shop the following morning or for the remainder of the week. She tried calling his cell phone, but it went immediately to his voice mail.

George asked her after a few days if Jefferson had gone away on another trip since he had not been into the shop. She made an excuse about some family business he was taking care of out of town.

Abby contacted the couple who had been inquiring about the china and the bedroom furniture. They were overjoyed to hear from her and made an appointment with her for the end of the week. She promised to not display any of the items until they had looked at them first.

She tried to keep her mind occupied with the shop. It was difficult to stop thinking about the vision they had seen. She had such a strong feeling there was much more to the quarrel that had resulted in a duel. She spent her days working with George and managing to find customers for most of the added items she had found at the estate sale. George did not ask any further about Jefferson's whereabouts. He did notice that Abby looked very bothered by something. He remained a gentleman and did not voice any of his concerns.

He thought they might have had a personal disagreement. He hoped that was not the case but remained silent. He had a feeling it was more than just a lover's spat. Abby was not the kind of woman to get involved with anyone that she did not care about. He knew by her earlier behavior that she did have feelings for Jefferson. He hoped that Jefferson would show up at the shop by the end of the week but was disappointed when he did not.

He considered contacting Jefferson on his own but decided it might be best to remain quiet. He had seen Jefferson's temper a few times through the years and did not wish to have it coming his way.

When he worked for Jefferson's father, John, he had also seen signs of the temper that seemed to run in the family. It almost got him fired one day when he tried to intervene. That was when he decided to do his work and keep his opinions to himself. Otherwise, he would be unemployed, and he could not afford that to happen with a family to care for.

CHAPTER THIRTY-THREE:

The weekend passed by without any word from Jefferson. Abby drove by his house but did not see his car in the driveway. She finally decided to call him Sunday evening, but again it went straight to his voice mail.

Monday morning, she arrived at the shop and parked her car just as she saw his car coming down the street. She waited for him to park and walked over to his car. "Morning Abby. How are you on this beautiful day?" he asked.

She hesitated and finally replied, "I am fine thank you. George and I were beginning to be genuinely concerned over your absence. Are you feeling better?" He turned and smiled. She followed as he entered the shop. "I am simply fine, thanks for asking. I just had some business to attend to. I knew you both could handle everything at the shop without me. Besides, you are the new owner."

With that comment he walked over to George and Abby continued into the office. "Well, that was rather short and vague," she thought. When Jefferson walked into the office, he told her he was pleased to hear about the sales they had. "Looks like you were able to find buyers for all the latest items we purchased at the sale." She told him about the couple showing up on Friday. "They purchased the china and all the bedroom furniture we brought in. They were extremely satisfied with the prices and the furniture. I gave them the china set at half price since they purchased so many other larger pieces."

Jefferson nodded and told her that was a good idea. "They will give our shop, or Your shop, a complimentary review. When others hear about how accommodating you were they might decide to check us out also. Again, Abby, you have shown great marketing skills."

The day continued with Jefferson in the same strange mood. He waited on a few people and then announced he was leaving for the remainder of the day. Abby stood and watched as he walked out the door. She glanced over at George, and he looked as surprised as she did. She could not understand what had happened to the pleasant man she knew. This recent version of Jefferson was extremely quiet. He did not engage in any pleasantries while he was in the shop.

He had not asked her about looking through more of the old newspapers. She wondered if she should venture over to continue the search on her own but decided she would wait for Jefferson.

The following days at the shop were the same. Jefferson would come in for a brief time in the morning and then disappear for the rest of the day. He would say hello and goodbye to her and George and that was all the conversation they heard from him.

She knew George was starting to wonder what was going on, but he did not ask her any questions about Jefferson's strange behavior. Abby finally decided to confront Jefferson and find out exactly what the problem was.

She told George to lock up when the day was over. She said she would do the deposit the next morning. When she walked out George stood in the shop watching her drive away. He just shook his head and went back to his work.

Abby drove to Jefferson's house. When she saw his car parked in the rear of the property she pulled in the driveway. She made her way up to the front door and rang the bell. After a few minutes she saw him coming towards her. "Abby. What are you doing here?" he asked.

"I came to talk to you Jefferson. I thought since we are away from the shop, we could speak in private about whatever is troubling you. I am very worried about you." He moved away from the door so she could come inside.

"Please come in. We can go into the study to talk." She noticed how tired he looked. There were dark circles under his eyes and his clothes looked like they had not been changed for a few days.

"Please sit down. Can I get you anything?" She nodded. "No. Thank you. Jefferson, please talk to me. What is going on with you?" He sat down across from her and did not answer for a few minutes.

"Abby. What I am going to tell you will be a shock. I am afraid it will give you a quite different impression of myself and my family." She smiled and told him whatever he was going to tell her would not make any difference. She had seen what a kind and compassionate man he had been. She felt like he could still be that same man once he unburdened himself of whatever was so heavy on his mind.

CHAPTER THIRTY-FOUR:

"I do not know exactly where to begin. I decided to go back to the Town Hall and look through more of the papers by myself. I went through most of the films for that same year without finding any more articles. The first film for the following year contained some remarkably interesting information."

She listened as he explained about what he found on that film and newspaper. There was an article referring to Elizabeth Hemmings. It was an obituary notice. It told that her body had been found hanging in the barn on her estate. She had committed suicide.

Abby gasped. "Oh my. That poor woman." Jefferson continued. "Yes, she was. The paper stated that she was survived by her infant son who would be raised by her family. I did not find any other references to her or her son in any of the other films."

They sat looking at each other. Abby reached for his hand, but he pulled it away. "I still do not understand why you are so upset," she told him. "Please Abby. Just listen and you will understand soon enough. After I returned home, I started hunting through the house. I finally found my answers when I searched the closet in my father's bedroom. There were some loose floorboards in his closet which I noticed. When I pried them up, I found a wooden box hidden there. Inside I found many photos of a young boy. They were photos of Elizabeth Hemmings son."

Abby sat and listened as he continued with his story. "The boy had been raised by her father and mother after her death. His name was Arthur. He was named for his father, Captain Arthur Warren."

Abby tried to understand what he told her. "Elizabeth and the captain had an affair. She got pregnant. Is that why the captain had the duel with your grandfather? Was the baby his son?"

Jefferson did not answer her questions but continued with his explanation. "I also found a letter with the photos. It was addressed to my grandfather, and it was from Elizabeth. It told him about the paternity of the baby she had given birth to. The baby was Captain Warren's son. They had been in love for quite some time. Her family would not give their approval for a wedding since Elizabeth was young. Also, they did not approve of her marrying the captain of a fishing boat. They wanted her to marry my grandfather and tell him the child was his. She refused to follow their wishes."

"In the letter she explained that she had become overwhelmed with the death of the captain. She told him about her family's wishes to have her marry him since he was a wealthy and important man in the community of Cobble Bay. She also said that was never going to happen and he should forget about the feelings he had for her."

He then told Abby that there was another small newspaper clipping telling of Elizabeth's suicide. She had left a note saying she was taking her life so she could join her only true love, Captain Warren.

Abby sat amazed at the information Jefferson had uncovered. "How can you be certain this is all true?" He looked at her with tears in his eyes. "I have an elderly aunt, my father's sister who is still living. She resides in a nursing home in Boston. I went to see her, and she told me the truth about the duel. My grandfather was the one who initiated the duel with the captain. He had been courting Elizabeth for quite some time with hopes of making her his bride. He found out that Elizabeth was going to run away with Captain Warren. When my grandfather heard that he went out of his mind with rage. He was an expert shooter far better than the captain. Elizabeth did not hear about the duel until it was over. She arrived at the field to find her lover's dead body still laying in a pool of blood on the cold ground. My aunt said she had known about the baby but had not told the captain. She planned to tell him after they were wed."

Abby understood now why Jefferson was so upset. His grandfather proved to be a very desperate man when it came to loving Elizabeth. He had been very possessive of her while they courted. Her father was impressed with John's money and prestige in the town, so he overlooked the abusive behavior with his daughter. He had hopes of an impressive dowry to come into his hands after the wedding. That was his major concern. When John learned of the pregnancy, he became enraged with Elizabeth. After a short courtship he married Jefferson's grandmother Analissa. They later produced a child who was Jefferson's father John.

Elizabeth's father was the person who brought the trunk to the shop. He had locked the wedding garments and the pistols inside. He felt that John would be able to dispose of the contents before anyone could find out the truth about the duel. John agreed to take possession of the trunk to save his own reputation. He never mentioned any of this story to Jefferson's father. There was gossip in the town about Elizabeth's suicide. Her parents and family could not believe she was the kind of woman who would leave her child. When the note was discovered in her desk, the case was closed and declared a suicide. No further investigation took place.

The trunk had remained in the attic of the shop for many years. Jefferson's father never tried to locate the key and assumed it had been destroyed so no one could open the trunk.

Abby sat quietly after hearing Jefferson's explanation. She was not sure how to approach him after hearing the truth about his grandfather. Finally, she offered a suggestion. "Jefferson. I know this story has taken you by surprise. Why don't you take some time for yourself away from the shop and the memories. Take another trip that will clear your mind. George and I can manage without you. For a while anyway."

Jefferson smiled at her after hearing her words. "Abby. I do care for you deeply. I had hopes of having a future with you. Now after uncovering the truth about my family's secret, I think we should spend some time apart. I know I have a temper just like my father and grandfather. I do not want that to become a problem for us if we take our relationship any further."

Abby had been thinking about his story and agreed that he had shown similar traits. She had been concerned about his lack of control when it came to personal situations. "You are correct. A trip will help you to put things into perspective about your family. Even some counseling would help. I do care for you Jefferson. However, after the life I had with Joseph I do not want to make the same error in judgement. When you return, we can take things slow and see what the future holds for us." He took her hand and kissed it. "Thank you for being so understanding Abby."

Jefferson walked her to the door. He wanted to grab her into his arms and not let her go. He knew she was correct about his needing to get away and deal with all that he had learned about his family. It would not be fair to continue their relationship until he could put the past behind him and move forward without any hesitation.

Abby reached up and kissed him lightly on the cheek. "Please take care of yourself. Send us a post card and let us know that you are all right." He nodded and watched as she drove away.

He decided to contact his travel agent the next day and have her make travel arrangements for him. He hoped travelling would put the doubts he had out of his head. He had definite plans to destroy the additional papers he had found. There would be no positive proof to show Elizabeth's death was in fact not a suicide. He would try to come to terms with the true facts he had learned concerning his grandfather.

He hoped he could come back to Abby with a clear mind and conscience someday.

CHAPTER THIRTY-FIVE:

Abby arrived back at her house. She felt drained of any emotion. It had been difficult to tell Jefferson to leave but she knew it was the correct thing for him. When she entered the front door, she could still feel a chill inside. She looked around but saw nothing. She had listened to Jefferson's explanation of all the evidence he had uncovered regarding his grandfather and Elizabeth. There was still one doubt in her mind. If the apparition they had seen was in fact Elizabeth, what did she want from them. Abby knew there were still some unanswered questions about Elizabeth and Jefferson's grandfather. She hoped she could uncover more answers regardless of how difficult it might be. She felt that Elizabeth wanted the truth to be discovered.

She walked to the den and put another log on the fire. She sat down and noticed the light blinking on her phone. Her daughter had left her a message and after hearing it she decided to return the call.

"Hello mother? I have tried to reach you a few times. Is everything all right with you and Jefferson?" Abby sat for a moment before she answered Cassie. "Hello sweetheart. Sorry I missed your calls. I am fine. There has been a lot going on and I would like to explain it all to you. Just not tonight. I am tired. It has been an exhausting day. I promise I will explain everything. Please do not worry about me. I am fine. I will call you later in the week."

Cassie told her mother that was fine and after a short chat about her pregnancy they ended the call. Abby went to her bedroom and changed into some comfortable clothes and returned to the kitchen. She poured herself some wine and spent the remainder of the evening sitting by the fire. Her thoughts were of Jefferson. She knew how strong her feelings had become for him.

She had been ready to take their relationship to the next level physically. Her body yearned for the closeness of another. It had been some time since she had felt any arousal from a man's touch. When she had seen how emotional Jefferson had become after finding the truth about his family, she knew it would not be wise for them to become intimate at this time. He needed to deal with his feelings before he would be ready to get further involved with her.

She had been hurt so many times by Joseph through the years. His attitude towards her and their children had almost broken her. She had been able to work through his rejection for the sake of their children. She was not ready to get involved with another man who had similar personal issues to deal with. She did care about Jefferson, but she had also learned to care about herself. She wanted and needed a man who could commit totally to her and their future together. She knew that Jefferson could not at this time. She hoped that the future would heal him, and they could someday be together.

While she waited for the future, she felt she deserved she would manage the shop. With George's help she knew they could turn the Antique shop into a much more profitable business. That would be her future. She was the owner and had come to love everything about the shop. The classic items they sold were precious to her. She loved sizing up the customers and putting them with the exact pieces they desired for their homes. She was good at it, and it gave her great satisfaction to see happy people leave with their purchases.

She finally went to bed in the early morning hours. She slept restlessly for a brief time. When she woke to see the sunny day, she felt renewed. She showered and dressed for her day. Grabbing a container of hot coffee, she drove to the store to begin her new adventure. She waved at George who was waiting for her by the front door. She knew he deserved an explanation of Jefferson's strange behavior. She was not certain just how much she would tell him.

"Good morning miss," he said as she walked up to the door. "Hello George. How are you today?" He smiled. "Fine. Looks like another beautiful fall day." She nodded. "Yes George, it certainly does."

They walked inside the shop together. Abby went to the office to get the deposit for George. He waited by the door and when she handed him the bank bag, he tipped his hat and walked outside to do the banking. Abby sat down at the big desk and smiled to herself.

"Yes George. It looks like another beautiful day."

TO BE CONTINUED.....